The Sheriff's Mistletoe Bride

The Sheriff's Mistletoe Bride

Destiny's River

Debra Holt

TULE
PUBLISHING

The Sheriff's Mistletoe Bride
Copyright© 2025 Debra Holt
Tule Publishing First Printing, October 2025

The Tule Publishing, Inc.

First Publication by Tule Publishing 2025

Cover design by Lee Hyat Designs

ISBN: 978-1-967678-79-2

The Sheriff's Mistletoe Bride....

This is the third book in my Destiny's River series. If you have followed the Parker siblings through the first two, you will find that this book has Matt Parker as its hero. Matt and his young daughter Jillie now have their own story.

It was fun to write this book because of the warm sibling relationships between the brothers and the sisters. And in this story, I introduce readers to Ally, a city girl with a much different family background than the Parkers. She will make her way to Destiny's River in order to honor the wishes of a woman very dear to her. But it's Christmas… and we know magic can happen and especially in Destiny's River, Texas.

The dedication of this book is to say a HUGE thanks to the incomparable team of ladies at Tule Publishing. I may not say it enough, but all of you are special and have taken such good care of my characters and their stories over the years. I appreciate you more than you know, and it is time that I dedicate a special holiday story to each of you.

With my sincere gratitude and best wishes to each of you… you are all amazing!

Debra Holt

Chapter One

"I HATE CHRISTMAS."

Ally didn't say the words out loud. She never said them out loud. Think of the reaction they would get from so many others. But then…maybe not so many? She took a silent survey of the faces around her as each sat in their own little worlds. They perched on cold plastic benches, eyes not meeting others, their shared conveyance a subway car clicking, clacking, zooming along in the darkened world beneath the crowded New York City streets above them.

A cocoon that was its own world until one had to fight others to return to the concrete jungle above it. Then the race would begin again…humans scurrying to their destinations, day after day, night after night. Speakers blared their canned holiday music. Even though they were just at the beginning of November. Were they planning on skipping the poor turkeys' day altogether this year? Already storefronts glittered and gleamed, enticing others to come inside and spend their hard-earned money on gifts that were touted to be *must-haves* in a world that already had too much.

Yes, what if I just spoke the truth out loud? Would anyone care? Would anyone hear? What difference would it make? Ally pulled her long brown tweed jacket closer around her and sank her chin farther into the folds of the cheap scarf she had wrapped around her neck. Just another layer of cocoon against the world around her.

She walked with her head down, eyes on the cracks in the sidewalk that was under constant construction, or destruction, depending upon the neighborhood. Her neighborhood consisted of a three-block row of identical cracker boxes...at least that is how she thought of them in her mind as she looked at their square front and long, narrow lengths. They each had six steps up to the door, which then opened on a tiny hallway of two doors and an even smaller stairway to floors two, three, and four. She was on the third floor. And she shared the two-bedroom apartment with its one bathroom, and the living room/kitchen/dining room combo that was really grand-sounding, but the dining was two TV trays in front of the small two-person settee and old leather rocker/recliner that had seen better days twenty years before. In fact, the whole group of their furnishings came from the same place as her meager wardrobe...the neighborhood thrift store.

Thankfully, she had reached the steps just as a light mist began to fall from graying clouds that had threatened most of the afternoon. The night was going to be another dark, cold one, which only added to her spirit level...in the wrong direction. Ally made the measured climb up the threadbare carpet of the staircase just as she traversed the streets on the way to and from her workplaces, by autopilot. She was thankful she had already gotten the small grocery list of staples two days ago. Her hand rummaged around inside her shoulder bag for the key ring. The new weight on it paused her fingers.

A stab of sadness enveloped her, and she allowed her forehead to rest against the chipped gray paint of the front door of what had been her home for the last eight years. Ally remembered the days when she would not hesitate to open the door, step through and be greeted with a warm smile and inquiries as to how her day had gone. The smell of home cooking would fill the tiny four-room apartment, and she would feel a warmth grow within her and a smile could not be held back.

Her hand paused on the doorknob. The key was inserted but first came a deep breath to help steel herself against the wave of painful memories that had never stemmed in the four weeks since the warmth and light had gone from the tiny corner of the world, she had called home. Nothing would change the inevitable so best to get it over. Ally stepped through the doorway and shut the door behind her with a loud thud. The three locks were turned, and her keys went into the small ceramic shell that sat on a table beside the door. Her shoulder bag went onto the peg on the wall behind the table. The sound of claws on the tile floor from the small kitchen put a smile on her face and she turned to widen the smile into a grin. The little furry missile was headed straight for her, ears flapping like dual flags, tail waving side to side so fast that its bottom was fairly lifted off the ground in its fervor.

Ally clapped her hands and then the furry missile was scooped off the floor and buried in her arms. The dog's wiggling body made her laugh. She liked to think that just maybe the dog was trying to make up for the absence of its mistress. Silly notion perhaps, but then maybe not. Annie

Pickett had worked her special magic over people in her life, and Ally wouldn't doubt she had instructed her little Teddy to make sure to look out for her when she left them. Would the pain ever be less sharp in her chest? People said it would. But so far, she could prove them wrong.

"Were you a good boy today? Did you play with your buddies in the park? Let's find the note and see what Laura has to say." Laura Reyes was a teen neighbor from the fourth floor. She and her mother were good neighbors, and they looked out for each other. Ally settled on the faded sofa and Teddy sat patiently awaiting the verdict at her feet.

"Teddy was a sweetheart today." Ally glanced over at the dog who seemed to have an angelic smile on his face at the news. "However, he had a problem with the English bulldog from across the park, who doesn't seem to fit in too well with the rest. Teddy finally grabbed his ball and ran away with it. I gave chase and we delivered it back to the pouting dog and his stuck-up owner who said Teddy was a mongrel ruffian. Teddy got an extra doggie treat when we got home because he isn't a mongrel ruffian. Hope he won't be grounded from playtime tomorrow? See you at the usual time," Ally read.

"You might not be a pure breed, but you have more class than that snooty bulldog. And he is almost twice your size at that." Her gaze softened on the mix-matched animal. That was how she always described the dog in her mind…but never out loud. Annie wasn't too certain of what breed…make that *breed*…might have come into play in Teddy's pedigree. His ears resembled floppy fur flags when he was in motion. His body was short and compact like a terrier; his tail was bushy like a fox's. There was a perpetual smile on his face that held big black button eyes that could melt anyone's heart. And Teddy had owned Ally's in total since the moment they'd laid eyes on each other all those years ago.

"You should try to remember that you aren't a playground bully. At your age, you need to leave that to some of the other pups." Then a dark thought crowded into the moment. She had lost Annie too soon in her thinking. And that left her Teddy. He wasn't a spring chicken either in dog-to-human years. In human years, he would be in his eighties. But she wiped the rest of that thought away. *Don't borrow trouble, girl.* She could hear Annie's admonishment even now. More than once those words had been sent her way.

"Tomorrow, you get an extra hour with Laura," Ally said, folding the note and standing. Teddy began to dance around. He knew the routine. And it was solidified as he followed on Ally's heels toward the front door. She took down her warmer insulated jacket and pulled it on. Her good shoes were traded for serviceable boots with a thin layer of inside warmth. The outside fake leather could better handle the wet streets of the evening. She checked her pockets for gloves and found them. When she reached next for the leather leash, the dog at her feet added a couple of twists and even a slight hop. Ally bent and snapped the leash to the collar. She laughed at the joy of the animal and hoped to capture some of it on their walk. The last item she added was her bright red knitted cap that was her birthday gift last year and handmade by Annie. She tucked the small songbook inside her purse, and it then went over her shoulder and the pair were ready. It was all Teddy could do to maintain composure to follow her slower steps out of the apartment. But it was he who led the way down the stairs with her laughter following him.

Darkness had fallen like an early theater curtain call across the city dubbed the 'City That Never Sleeps.' Although in her little corner of that world, Ally knew that at least it slowed down after dark when people arrived home and suppers had begun, homework was started, and tired feet were allowed to slow before the next shift. In her case, they were off to the tiny stone-fronted church three blocks away. It had become a weekly ritual for the last four years of her life. She often accompanied Annie to services following much encouragement from the woman after she had accepted her generous offer of a roof over head one rainy afternoon. It turned out to be a godsend, a miracle of sorts, that their paths had crossed in that moment. And there have been more such moments over the years. Annie had taught her to believe and have faith, and to be able to use the strength she had built inside to be the impetus to reach for more than she thought she could ever expect. Ally knew she had more work to do on that score, but she would have to do it alone now.

Thursday evenings were the time she was expected to be at the small church. The routine was automatic for her and Teddy. They would enter down the flight of steps at the side of the building. Down a short hallway filled with coatracks for outerwear, then the smell of hot chocolate would greet them, fresh-baked cookies still in ovens would soon be ready for their breaks or after the choir rehearsals. Ally knew she was lucky to be able to have Teddy join her but the students in her children's choir had vocally pleaded with Pastor Nesbitt and the man had succumbed to Teddy's big eyes with his own plea. Teddy had a box with a comfy pillow underneath the piano in the small rehearsal room. He took his spot and only came out at break time when Ally gave permission. Then he enjoyed doggie biscuits while the humans had the cookies.

Annie would often come along and sit in the back, eyes closed, smile on her face, as she enjoyed the sweet angelic voices learning the hymns of her own childhood. She had given Ally the courage to say yes when the pastor had asked one day, two years ago, to take over the choir. She had taken a big step in her mind. And had been rewarded with such joy ever since. But what she still found hard to believe was that others found her voice to be worthy of attention. While she would use it to teach the children and to hide behind others in the adult choir when needed, there was no way she would agree when the pastor would ask her to perform a solo at Sunday service. *Baby steps.*

The group of eight students, ranging from five to nine in age, three boys and six girls, came bustling in, with hugs for Ally and pats on the head for Teddy, who then retreated under the piano. Maggie Davis, a retired schoolteacher and their volunteer pianist came in soon after and it was down to business. Ally loved this part of her day, and it was why Thursdays were special. Although she was acutely aware of the empty chair at the back of the room. Or maybe it wasn't. She tried to think along those lines, but it was still too raw a loss of such a magical and strong spirit.

"The voices of angels! That's what I hear in this room,

Miss Ally." The short, rotund man stepped into the room on the last stanza of the song right before cookie break. His words trailed behind the announcement of the cookies and milk being served in the dining hall. With a smile and nod at the children's expectant look in her direction, the room was quickly emptied of little bodies.

"Thank you, Mr. Jacobs. Forgive the thundering herd that just heard the call to the goodies. They are all treasures to be sure."

"Indeed, they are and so have you been to them." He smiled as he came to stand beside the piano. "Beautiful accompaniment also." Of course, he was a little partial as the pianist was his sister.

She stood and shook her head. "Well, the pianist needs some sustenance also. I'll leave you two to follow the herd and myself." She left them.

"You aren't in the mood for cookies?" Ally asked as she noted the man seemed to have something on his mind as he continued to stand with a thoughtful look on his features. Annie always referred to it as his 'lawyerly look.'

"In a few minutes," he responded. "I do need to have a few words with you. About Annie's last wishes and her will."

Ally felt a sudden sense of losing her appetite as her stomach tightened. It was a natural reflex she had developed, which often heralded not so good news. *First law of preservation...make the first move.*

"What's the bad news? No use waiting on that."

His small smile twitched a bit under his mustache. "I just wanted to make certain you could still make the formal reading tomorrow. And the specific instructions to you will follow."

"Yes, I took a couple of hours off. I'll be there on time."

"That's good. And don't worry, my girl. Annie was indeed of a sound mind and thought everything out to the last detail. You know you can always trust her to know best. Now I am going to grab a cookie and my granddaughter and get home. Have a good sleep tonight and be safe going home." He gave her a fatherly pat on the arm and left her.

Ally sat down on the piano bench. Teddy sensed something and moved to sit at her feet, his eyes watching her movements. With one hand she rubbed over his soft fur and tickled behind one of his floppy ears. "It's silly to wish that tomorrow was behind us, I know. We will get through it. Same as always." She just wished she felt as certain as she was trying to sound out loud. Annie had always had the ability to sound confident and look for the silver linings and all the good things. Ally wished she could have bequeathed to her those attributes in her will. Why hadn't they had more time for her to learn more from Annie? Annie…the woman who had risked a chance on taking an orphan from the streets of New York under her wing, giving her a roof, a job, and an opportunity for a better life.

Ally had left that uncertain, frightened mouse of her young self behind thanks to Annie's tutelage. Only she hadn't taught her by book lessons and tests. She had taught her by living life each day…facing good and bad and making the best choices. When she failed, she learned from it. And she never repeated her mistakes again. And facing another night in an empty apartment with just herself and Teddy was only the beginning of yet another lesson.

Sleep wasn't all that much after they returned home.

With Teddy on constant watch from his bed beside hers, she didn't close her eyes until the early morning hours. Arriving at her first job as cashier at a popular bakery and café right off Broadway, she felt the effects by mid-morning. Then she had to rush to be on time to meet the five-year-old twins she did after-school sitting with at one o'clock. By the time their aunt arrived to take over since Ally had arranged to leave before six due to her meeting with Mr. Jacobs, she was filled with both a headache and a draining tiredness. She knew a lot of it had to do with anxiety that overshadowed the lack of sleep and uncertainty of what was to come. The secretary showed her right to Mr. Jacobs's office upon her arrival.

"Come in, my dear. Have a seat. You are punctual as always." He spoke from behind his massive oak desk strewn with papers and open law books and empty coffee cups. "What would you like Clara to get you? Coffee, soft drink..."

"I'm fine. I just need to hear what you have to tell me."

"I see. I can understand. There are several things to get through so let's just jump right in." He slid his glasses from the top of his head to rest on the bridge of his nose. He picked up the top paper from the stack in front of him and cleared his throat.

He read the brief will about Annie being of sound mind et cetera and Ally listened to each word. Then he paused and she knew that the real items were about to begin.

"I'll summarize a lot of this, and you will have a copy of all these papers handed to you by Clara when you leave. But let's get to the main points. You are her beneficiary of all she left. There are a few requests of odds and ends she left to certain acquaintances and those will be dealt with. I am the executor, and my office will help you in any way we can."

"She left me her apartment?" Ally managed to ask that question for her own peace of mind. But it didn't elicit the answer she hoped.

"She left you instructions on what she wanted done with it. While it would certainly be correct for you to think that it was part of her estate, she left instructions to you for what she wanted. She wants the apartment to be sold. In fact, she had already secured a person who wanted to give the asking price and take possession of it as soon as possible."

"What am I to do? Where do I go? I don't..." She stopped when he held up his hand.

"Annie knew that you would not need the apartment, but you would need the money from its sale plus her savings to handle her wishes for what she needed you to do. I will simply list it and then we can discuss the questions you might have."

Ally fell silent. Her world had imploded even more than she had dreaded. And there was more to come.

"Annie's cremated remains are to be taken, by you, to Destiny's River, Texas. I believe she had often thought of it and shared her feelings about it with you?"

Ally could only nod in agreement. How was she to make this happen?

"As you know, she has an automobile stored on the outskirts of the city. I believe she gave you driving lessons in it. Anyway, I have seen that it is in top condition and ready to transport you and her to Texas. She ensured that you would have more than enough funds to take the trip, and then to set you up for a year once you leave Destiny's River...should you want to do so. She wrote instructions as to what you were to do once you arrived there. And she also left another letter for you to read in hopes of understanding why she placed this...her final wish on this earth...in your trusted hands.

"She never had children or any family to speak of over these many years, until there was you. We had many talks over that time, she and I, and I can say with all candor that she saw you as her family. She was proud of you, how hard you worked, how much you cared for others and herself, and she wanted nothing but to leave you well able to continue to find your own dreams. But first, you'll take her where her heart never left. To the place she always considered home even though she was so far from it in miles. Rest this evening and read her words and then call me. You and I will begin this journey to send you on your path to Texas."

It seemed with each step she took from the lawyer's office to the subway...the same word kept repeating in her head. *Texas.* She had listened to the stories Annie told of her life there. It always seemed like a far-off country in Ally's mind. One she never imagined ever to see. Now she was expected to make the trip on her own to this foreign land. It was so far away from what she knew. From anyone who knew her or she them. But it was Annie's request of her. The last one she would ever make. And she hadn't ever asked much of herself while she was alive. But Ally owed her so much. Taking her to where she'd longed to be for so many years. And then leaving her there.

It would be very hard. But she would do this last thing

for the only person who had showed her what it was she wanted...to have memories like Annie did of a beautiful place where love grew, and people were welcomed, and families could flourish and grow. *Texas.* Would it welcome her, too?

Chapter Two

"CATNIP. THAT'S WHAT you are."

Sheriff Matthew Parker shouldn't be surprised by much that his ten-year-old daughter might come up with, but her words as she slipped into her seat belt, and looked smugly over at him, made him stop in his tracks. "Where did you get that from and what are you doing repeating such craziness? And what do you know about catnip?"

She rolled her eyes and took a quick sip from the straw in her chocolate milkshake. "Come on, Dad. Everyone says that. I even heard my aunts both say it. And it means that all the single girls in this town think you are hot stuff. You need a wife, and they are lining up to apply. That's catnip to them, Dad."

Matt shook his head. "It's about time I have a conversation with my sisters. The rest of the town I can't do much about, but those two need to remember you are an impressionable child with big ears!" He turned the key and the engine in his truck roared to life. He squelched the urge to hit the loudspeaker button on his official vehicle and announce once and for all to the world that he, Matt Parker, was not in the market for a wife and when he was, it was his business and not theirs. He often wondered if he could back that up with writing tickets to those who repeated such garbage.

"It's okay. But they do have something. You aren't getting any younger, Dad. And I could use another girl in the house. You know, to help me win arguments about clothes and stuff."

Those words caused him to shoot a quick look in his daughter's direction. Had he missed something? Neglected something? It wasn't easy being the town's sheriff and a single dad of a precocious and way too smart for her own good female child. Luckily, they came to a halt at a red light.

"Have I missed something? Have I not done something right? Is there something we need to talk about or ask one of your aunts about?"

Jillie shook her head. "Relax, Dad. You are great…ninety-eight percent of the time."

"Only ninety-eight percent? What have I missed?"

"You don't get a perfect score…no parent does. Now, maybe if you let me go to bed later once in a while during the week…that might push you up to a ninety-nine."

"Guess I will just have to be imperfect because the answer is still no way. Nice try, Jilliebean."

"And Dad, we need to discuss you using that name for me when we're around others."

"Others?"

"My friends and stuff."

He cast a sidewards glance at his daughter. "Stuff would be boys?"

"Dad! I didn't say that."

"I did. And just remember, you are not dating until you're thirty."

The famous eyeroll appeared. "By thirty, you will be really old and won't know what I'm doing anyway."

"Well, you will always be Jilliebean to your family and we..."

"And we're *here*, Dad. Stop and let me out." She pointed out the fact while grabbing up her bag and unsnapping her seat belt. He managed to pull to the curb and the door opened to let her exit, her usual can't-wait-another-moment to be off and running to the next item on her schedule. In this case it was choir practice at the church. "Bye, Dad, and yes I know Aunt Tori will pick me up." That was thrown over her departing shoulder with a fast wave and then she was halfway up the steps of the side door of the building.

What had happened to his calm, little, angelic baby girl? His ten-year-old was going on twenty at times. And that meant the aforementioned infamous thirty wasn't far behind. He grimaced at the thought. He needed coffee.

The bell above the door jangled as a countrified butler of sorts to alert the arrival of yet another guest into the welcoming atmosphere of Tillie's Café. The small country diner had been in this same building, same location on the corner of a street bordering the town's square, across from the courthouse, in view of the sheriff's office, for over five decades. Matt never knew a time when opening that door that the bell didn't jangle, that the aroma of fresh-baked bread didn't rouse the stomach, nor that the smiling shout of welcome that the owner met each guest with whether they might see you a few times each day or not didn't greet him. No one was a stranger in Tillie's.

Before Matt could take his place on one of the red leather swivel seats lining the long Formica-covered bar, there was a steaming mug of hot coffee poured and sat in the spot for him. The woman smiled as he took his seat. "What'll it be today? Biscuits and gravy or a freshly baked cinnamon roll?"

"I had breakfast at home this morning, Tillie."

"Right. I'm sure you fixed a real nice one for Jilliebean and yourself. And again, I will ask—biscuits and gravy or cinnamon roll?" The smile on her face told him that she had this conversation so often with him over the years that they both knew it was just an old habit by now.

"Roll, please." He knew when to call it quits and he responded with a sheepish hint of a grin. A sip of the still-hot coffee made him set the mug back down. At the same time a slap on his back brought his attention to the man who slid into the seat beside him. Matt nodded at his brother-in-law, Cade Lockwood.

"What brings you into the big city here?"

"The auction over at the Scotts' place. Your sister has her eye on Mary's china cabinet. And I thought I might check out that new combine he was so proud of."

"Thought you already had a couple of those?" Matt asked, already knowing what was going on with this sudden interest in the new equipment.

"And that's about the same interest you have in that workbench and tools you already told Spence you wanted to be sure and get a bid on." He dished it right back to the uniformed man beside him.

"Well, I just hope there's a good turnout at the auction of townspeople who are like-minded. With Dave's sudden death, Mary needs all the extra funds she can get. And hopefully, she'll get a real good price on their land. She's moving to Dallas to be closer to her daughter, so she'll need a good start over there."

"Here you go, Sheriff Parker," the waitress said, placing the plate with the sweet confection in front of him and refilling his coffee mug from the pot in her other hand. He recognized her as one of Tillie's newest hires. Probably just over eighteen with a penchant for tight blouses and heavy makeup. Matt smiled his thanks and picked up his fork, ignoring the fact she continued to linger in front of him. A few seconds later, a napkin went beside his plate. He was about to reach for it when his glance caught the fact that something had been written on it. It was numbers and then he heard the low grunt of laughter from the man beside him. Matt drew his hand back and instead picked up his mug. He finished the last couple of sips and then reached for the check.

"You're forgetting something, aren't you?" The innocent look on his brother-in-law's face was not lost on him as being totally fake. The man nodded toward the scrap of napkin with the numbers.

"I'm not forgetting that I don't date teenagers." He reached for it and wadded it up and very nicely placed it in the trash bin by the cash register. This was noted by the waitress, and she gave him a look that told him exactly what she thought of him...and it wasn't complimentary.

Tillie accepted his check and payment with a shake of her head. "Sorry, Matt, but you're just—"

"Don't say it if it's catnip," he stated with a shake of his head. "My daughter already told me the latest gossip she has heard about her bachelor father and that was the operative word."

Tillie laughed and so did the man who stood ready to pay his check next. "It must be tough to be you, Sheriff Parker. So very in demand with the ladies."

The look he left them both with told them what he thought of the comment and their laughter. He paused briefly to check the street and traffic and then bounded across to the other side, throwing up a hand in response to one being sent his way out the window of a resident from his passing truck. Matt just needed to make it to his office, shut his door and find some peace and quiet.

"Here he is now, Mayor." His deputy spoke up as he stepped through the door and found his sister, the mayor of their town, standing in conversation with his chief deputy.

"Just one of the two people I want to speak to," he responded, leaving the obligatory good morning off the sentence. "Come into the office." He did not stop to see if she followed. Once behind his desk, the door clicked shut, and he looked up to see her poised in front of him, hands on hips.

"Please note that in spite of your current bad mood and the fact that your invite into your office just now sounded very close to an order…which I know you would never think of doing as the bottom line is in fact that I can remind you that one of the two of us in this room is the other's boss…but be that as it may, I will simply ask what the heck has gotten your shorts in a twist so early?"

"You and my other sister—otherwise known as Jilliebean's…Jillie's," he corrected, "aunts—should know better about repeating gossip in front of an impressionable child."

"Okay," she said, pushing up the sleeves of her sweater, "what is the infraction we're being accused of?"

"She informs me today in the car, that I am considered catnip...*catnip*, she said...which she said she heard via her aunts...and that certainly includes you. You both need to cease and desist educating my daughter on the latest gossip of this town.

It was very clear that Tori was trying very hard to maintain as much of her composure as possible. At least she knew that laughter in that moment would not help matters. "I can see where this might have gotten your morning off to a bad start."

"Bad start? No, that was accomplished when I was having a simple cup of coffee at Tillie's and her latest waitress—someone just barely out of childhood, a teenage man-eater—gave me her phone number along with my cinnamon roll."

She could contain it no longer and laughter escaped. "I am sorry," she tried to choke out between bouts of laughter at his expense, "but you bring this on yourself."

"And just how do you figure that one?"

"Face it, Matthew," she said, reining in her mirth, "you are a free man, in good health, with reasonably good looks, a nice house, good job, adoring sisters, and a beautiful little girl...and the population is a few hundred short of your variety of male at the moment considering the number of single females...and I'm just counting the ones of childbearing age."

"This has got to stop. Do you know how often I'm called to go to a house where a poor animal is stuck in a tree? Or there are strange noises in the basement? It's gotten to where I send someone else to the call and then I get complaints from the person who called for *me* to come to the scene. I should hire a wife and put myself out of misery." He sank down in his leather chair and closed his eyes.

There was silence. So much so that Matt ventured the opening of one eye to see if his sister was still in the room. She was. But there was an expression on her face that he knew and that made him come back to the present on full alert.

"No, Tori, I know what happens when you get that look and you start thinking and things happen, which usually don't go well for those involved."

She smiled. And that did nothing to reassure him. Just the opposite. "Matthew, you've just hit on a solution. Hire a wife. The single females will lose interest and move on to some other unsuspecting male."

Matt slowly shook his head. "Hire a wife. Is that in the yellow pages or do you just google it or—?"

"Oh, okay, smarty," she stopped him. "You wouldn't have to really hire someone and marry them. You could hire someone to say, be a girlfriend until the others cool down and find another guinea pig…so to speak."

"Again, I'm not sure where you hire one of those except someplace called an escort service…and I am fairly certain that would become the scandal of the century around Destiny's River."

She shrugged her shoulders and then moved to the door, hand resting on the doorknob when she turned to look at him. "It was just a suggestion. But you need to think of a way to take yourself off the market…or at least make people think that you are. I'll send you my bill for my advice. Bye!"

"Find a make-believe girlfriend…or just bite the bullet and sacrifice myself on the altar of catnip." He mumbled the words out loud to himself. And he knew that would not be an option. He had lost his wife even before their first anniversary when she bled out due to a physician's oversight in her postpartum care. He had raised Jillie from that moment. It had been just the two of them in their little family. He had hoped he had done his best…with the help of his siblings along the way. But it was tough. What if he chose the wrong person? What if Jillie ended up hurt? He felt the weight of that decision only grew stronger as the years passed.

Why did he allow his eldest sister to get inside his brain so easily? He would just have to hope for one of those Christmas miracles since the season would soon be upon them. If all else failed, maybe Santa would help a guy out.

Chapter Three

"HURRY, TEDDY," ALLY pleaded, "the rain is coming down harder now."

Such was their trip so far. Mile upon mile, traffic, and the quick stops for gas, and her standing and waiting upon Teddy to relieve himself and get back in the car. The rain had become an added bonus in Virginia. And it continued to travel with them along the same route.

Mr. Jacobs had been true to his word. The old two-door vehicle had been checked over at D and J Garage, a new set of tires put on, and their luggage was stowed. Teddy took his rightful place in the copilot's seat, and armed with maps and travel tips, and emergency numbers, the pair had set out for Texas…along with Annie's cremains secured in the back seat inside an even more secure box. Things went okay for the first couple hundred miles. Then the heater stopped working. So, Ally pulled out another sweater to layer under the one she already had on, and they continued.

Laura, who was Teddy's dogsitter after Annie's death, had given her an old hat that had belonged to her father before they departed. She had told her to put her hair up and wear it, and it would make people think it was a man traveling and not a lone girl and dog. Skeptical at first, it wasn't long before Ally had given it a try and somehow it did make her feel better.

Laura had also, along with Mrs. Jacobs, made sure she had a vast supply of homemade cookies to sustain her on the road. Mrs. Davis and the pastor's wife had supplied fresh fruit, apples and grapes and some chips, too. Ally was most grateful that she had Teddy as her companion. He listened to her break into song with the radio and seemed to approve of her musical selections. As the miles passed, Ally felt a strange lightness beginning to replace the trepidation she had felt as they saw New York City fade into the background. The note from Annie had instructions on the front that it wasn't to be read until they had arrived in Destiny's River. Using the map inside, she would know where to find the spot Annie had always planned to return to for her last rest.

Ally had planned to stop for their third evening in Memphis. That was a plus in the itinerary that had also been supplied by Mr. Jacobs's office. The hotel was quite lovely, and nothing she had imagined she would be staying in ever. It was next to Graceland. She had never traveled so much in her entire life. Annie had often entertained her with stories of the wonderful places she had been as a young girl and during her adult years. It was fitting that Ally ended up staying so close to the musical icon's history since Annie had been a fan to the end. Yet, it was also a sad reminder of those who were gone much too soon from those who loved them.

"What do you think she was thinking, Teddy?" The little dog's ears rose as he raised his head from the pillow it resided on. His button eyes regarded her in their almost human way. The click clacking of the roadway beneath their tires as they crossed the wide Mississippi below the old bridge had lulled the dog into a napping phase after they had pulled away from the hotel before the sun was too far up in the sky.

"I think she would have loved seeing all of this again," Ally supplied the answer herself. Teddy seemed to smile in agreement. A happy thought was soon followed by a semi-sad one as seemed to be the usual order of her memories. Crossing the state line, so to speak, in the middle of the bridge, they entered Arkansas. Just after noon, Ally pulled over for a quick bite, to exercise Teddy on his long leash, and stretch the kinks out of her body after being locked behind the steering wheel for so long. Walking along the path sheltered by such towering trees, she was amazed at their colors and size. Seeing the trees in Central Park was one thing but seeing them in a more natural environment was really amazing. Her admiration was cut short by the rumble of thunder in the distance.

"Come on, Teddy," she said with reluctance, "no time to waste now. The last thing we need is to be on the road in bad weather." She hoped that the storm was not headed in the same direction that they were. Once on the road, however, her hope was dashed. The dark clouds descended around them, the wind buffeting the small car, and raindrops began to pelt the windshield. The wiper blades were on high, but she was not having the best of luck in keeping the rain cleared from hindering her view of the road. The other drivers didn't seem to let the wind and rain convince them to slow down as they whizzed by and around her without a thought to the dangerous conditions. Her grip tightened on the steering wheel. Teddy was oblivious to the conditions. He was sound asleep as soon as the wipers began their constant swish-swash hypnotic sound.

Ally loosened her death grip on the wheel long enough to turn the radio on to make more sound to keep herself wide awake and vigilant. The only station that came through with any clarity was a country station and so she allowed George Strait to accompany her down the scary highway. Her first foray into country music had happened only the day before, but to her surprise she found it suited their travel, and it did grow on a person. The storm blew on around her; lightning became worse instead of better. Then she saw a sign informing her that Texas was just ahead. Maybe things would be better there? And that thought kept her mind occupied for the next few miles. Annie had told her so many stories of her life in that state that she felt almost like one might feel returning to a home after a long journey away from it. Her fanciful brain at work. How could you look forward to returning to a place you had never been to?

Another bridge was crossed and then the sign welcoming her to the state of Texas appeared through the rain and, as if on cue, the rain lessened and through the remaining drops on the windshield, she could see that sunshine shone ahead even though the rain was still falling. How strange! She shook her head. It was something she had not seen before. But she'd take it. The dark clouds had decided to stay in Arkansas. Whatever it was, Ally would take it as a good omen for their trip.

"Wake up, Teddy. Some copilot you are," she commented as she took an exit onto a side road to pull into a large convenience store/gas station. "Thanks for the help during that storm. Glad it didn't interrupt your nap." She grinned at her companion as he raised himself up and stretched, looking out the passenger side window to see where they were stopping. Her words did not faze him.

The tank full once again, she pulled into a parking place and then took Teddy out to enjoy the dog park that was part of the amenities of their stop. It seemed to be quite a popular spot judging by all the cars and people. Securing the dog back inside the car, she ventured inside to grab a snack and check out what was the draw for such a place. It was apparent the moment she walked in and was greeted with so many smiles and welcomes. Texas friendliness was certainly the order of the day. It wasn't just a slogan on a sign.

The aroma of the fresh-baked foods caught her attention and before long she had bought a sandwich and some other items. When she glanced at her watch, she was surprised at how time had gotten away from her as she browsed one aisle after another. After paying for her items, she returned to the car.

"Remind me to stop here again," she told Teddy as he eyed her sack. "This is quite a place. But I want to reach our destination before dark. And no, I didn't forget you." She smiled at him as she withdrew a dog chew bone from the sack between them. Teddy's body began to wag in anticipation as he watched her unwrap it and then present it to him on his blanket. He immediately went to work enjoying it.

"Okay, let's head due west and see this place Annie loved so much."

The road was definitely headed due west as the sun was intent on trying to beat them to the horizon ahead. Its brightness gave Ally a headache and the sunglasses were not much help with the constant glare. She was glad that she had some reprieve while maneuvering the traffic through Dallas and then through Fort Worth, both huge cities along her route. For someone who had little experience of highway driving, she was fast becoming attuned to it, but she still was on alert and followed the speed limits when very few others did.

"I guess the posted signs are just suggestions and not the rule," she joked to the animal beside her. But it was still nerve-racking for a person not used to driving much at all.

Once past the cities, the country became rolling hills, which were a change from the previous scenery. The GPS on her phone alerted her an hour later that she would need to turn off the main interstate and take a two-lane blacktop country road to the southwest. The hills became even more pronounced, and Ally's attention was divided more and more between the winding road and the changing countryside with its tall trees and intermittent creeks running through fields that appeared now and then. The grass was more brownish and tanner in this area, and here and there black cattle could be seen in pastures.

She was getting closer to what Annie had described over and over. *Sunbeams skipping off the trickling waters of a lazy creek as it rolls and circles stones in its path between massive roots of towering trees called cypresses that gravitated to the banks of rivers and lakes set amongst towering hillsides like blue gems.* Annie always sounded like a writer when describing the land she loved. Ally would often close her eyes and travel across the miles to the far-off landscapes of that distant place called Destiny's River, Texas.

She would rather think of those more pleasant moments than the ones in her life before she met Annie and everything changed for her. The time scale on her lifespan would come to be known in her mind as *Before Annie* and *After Annie.* That was how she cataloged her memories. Before Annie, she had been just one of thousands of runaways who ended up lost in the cement caverns of the city and never searched for. Losing her mother at age thirteen, she was then dumped on a street corner by her third stepfather when she was sixteen and too much of a troublemaker, according to him when he opened the car door and told her to get out.

She learned soon enough to leave tears out of things. They showed weakness. She had to be tough. And resourceful. Many times, she wanted to just give up, but something inside her would not allow that. And then one day, when the rain was pouring down and she was on a street corner trying to hand out the flyers she was getting ten dollars to distribute to passersby for a new pizza place, a woman had walked up and offered to give her twenty for the stack she had left. Then she had offered to buy Ally something to eat in the café two doors down.

Ally had been hungry and cold and wet. The hot meal sounded good. And that was how she met Annie Destino Pickett. Annie and she visited for an hour, then two, while the rain cleared. And then Annie handed Ally a card and told her about a job at a bakery four blocks away. She could go there and apply for a job and use Annie as a reference. She had nothing to lose, so she did. And she found herself employed. Then she found out the identity of the owner. It was Annie. Over the next few weeks, she was allowed to sleep in the back office of the business. Then about three months later, Annie offered her a room in her house. She had already observed how much Annie was respected by the neighborhood people who stopped in each day for homemade loaves of bread and pastries.

Ally took up the offer and that was how the pair of them became the first semblance of family that Ally had known in her life. A real family that was built on trust and love. She learned so much from Annie and the long talks they would share in the evenings. Annie had saved her. And only lately had Ally begun to feel that perhaps she might have brought something to Annie's life that she had searched for also. But thoughts of that life and Annie now were laced with a fragile heartache.

All things magical and heartbreaking and a glint of unshed tears often ended the tour of Annie's beloved memories. And thus, Destiny's River was the reason she had set off on a solo journey. Now, Ally was seeing it for herself. Would there be magic or… The next instant a flash of something she barely registered and a squeal of tires on pavement, mingled with a scream of shock that escaped from her throat as in slow motion the car left the roadway and became airborne as it topped the rise in the road. One hand gripped the steering wheel and the other instinctively shot out to shield the dog beside her and then it all went black.

☆

MATHEW PARKER WATCHED the scene unfolding in slow motion. Yet, it happened in a blinding split second of time.

One moment he opened his door to get out of his sheriff's vehicle while telling his daughter to stay in the car. But she moved faster than his words. He only got the scream of her name out before the squeal of brakes on pavement sounded as loud as a freight train in his brain. Then he began to run to where his child stood clutching the runaway kitten, frozen in her arms in terror. The child was a statue with bated breath. All this registered in his brain as he made it to the other side of the pavement to wrap Jillie in his arms and try to shield them all from the loud crunching of metal on gravel, and then a deafening silence followed.

Moving on adrenaline-spiked instinct, Matt carried his daughter swiftly across to the SUV and tucked her, still clutching the kitten, in the back seat while his hand went to his radio, and he called for ambulance and more help. Then he jumped into the front seat and put his lights on to bright flashing yellow as he quickly maneuvered the vehicle across the roadway to block both lanes. He was out and leaning into the back seat again.

"I have a lot of work right now to see if the people in that car need help and you need to not move from this vehicle. Understand what I just said? Say yes, Jillie."

First a nod and then a shaky voice responded: "Yes, Daddy. I'm sorry, Daddy."

"Just stay put. I love you." He dropped a swift kiss on her head and stepped back, shutting the door. The dad transformed into the official lawman with a job to do.

He went back across the road and was glad to see a pickup had pulled to a stop just a few yards down. He recognized the man as a rancher who lived a couple miles down the road. He could use him.

"Jason, if you would pull your vehicle across the top of the rise and until a patrol gets here? Shouldn't be long. Help is on the way."

"You got it, Matt," he responded with a shout and wave.

His attention turned to the vehicle and to his surprise and somewhat relief, he noted it hadn't rolled over but had slid down the steep side on the tall grass to land with its midsection lodged against two trees that seemed to have been placed there for this very situation. Whatever it was, he was glad of it. He slipped and slid a bit down the steep side until he reached the car. Glass had shattered due to the impact he assumed, so he was able to look inside and see there was one person, the driver presumably, a woman who was unconscious…he hoped. He had to pull more than a few times to get the door open wide enough to allow him to reach her hand and feel for a pulse. Relief and a thank you went upward, as she was still alive. Her head looked like it had taken a good hit and probably part of the missing windshield might be responsible for the gash on her forehead that was bleeding quite a bit. He knew from training and experience that head wounds always bled more and looked worse than they usually were, and he hoped this might be the case.

"Ma'am, are you okay? Can you hear me? Help is on the way. Can you hear me? Just stay still and answer if you can," he repeated and there was a faint flutter of eyelashes. A soft moan escaped her lips. She seemed to be in distress as she woke. He needed to keep her still until the ambulance arrived. There was a faint siren in the distance, and he hoped it was the ambulance in the lead.

"It's okay. Help is on the way. I'm not leaving until they get here."

"Teddy…I want Teddy. Where is Teddy? Annie…is she okay? Got to get them both." The words were hard to make out at first but were there others involved and not in the car?

"Who is Teddy? Who is Annie? Were they here in the car with you?"

"Yes! You must find them. Need them." Her lashes rose a bit in a wince of pain, and he saw bright blue glints through them. She was pleading. "Please find them. I was supposed to take care of them. I didn't see the child… Did I hit her? Oh no! Please help her…"

Matt laid a calming hand on hers and his was instantly gripped. "Help her…help them. Not me," she repeated.

"Help is here, and they will all be helped. But the little girl is just fine. She is safe."

"Thank God," she breathed and caught her breath on a painful note.

"I'm going to move now and let the paramedics help you."

Her hand gripped his tighter. "Find them please."

"I promise I'll find them for you. And I'll be right beside you as we get all of you to the hospital."

"Promise?" And there was a look in those blue eyes, now fully centered on him, that made any other word impossible to utter.

"I give you, my word." Then she was in the hands of the paramedics and her hand lost his. Mentally shaking himself, Matt backed out of the car and stood, his gaze scanning the area. He called out two of the four deputies. "You and

Bobby keep traffic under control," he said to one of the closer deputies. "Rich and Sandy, you search for a possible two others she mentioned…Teddy and Annie. Perhaps they were thrown from the car on impact when the glass shattered. Increase the search area."

The paramedics stabilized her and then moved her onto a stretcher. "Sheriff," one of them called out. "We can't be sure of internal injuries, and with the road under repairs closer to town, we're calling in the chopper."

Matt nodded. "Bobby…you guys secure a landing spot and set out a smoke flare for their approach for wind gusts on the road."

"We got it, Sheriff." His team was good. And in moments like this, they did their jobs without hesitation.

"We have searched high and low," Franny said, as she handed over a small purse. "Her ID is in there…Ally Jones from New York City. Long way from home. And there is no sign of any person other than her. We're taking the luggage and bags she has into the station for inspection. Maybe we'll know more then."

"Hey! I got Teddy over here," one of the officers called out. Matt and Sandy ran to the area. There, they found Teddy.

"It's a poor little dog," Sandy said, bending down to speak softly to him. "Looks like a broken bone maybe but really scared. His collar has Teddy on it."

"One mystery solved. Keep searching the area for anything or anyone else. Load the dog into the back of my vehicle and I'll drop him over at Doc's before I get to the hospital. You guys know what to do here."

They nodded and Franny gently transported the dog to

the SUV. He called after her, "And tell my daughter to keep her hands and that cat away from the dog." Franny nodded.

The sound of blades beating air could be heard in the distance. He walked to the stretcher where the supine body of the woman looked even smaller under the white sheet. Her face was almost as pale. Matt's hand rested on her lower arm.

Those blue eyes tried to focus better on him. There was a silent plea in them.

"We have Teddy. I'm going to take him myself to the vet…who is really good. He may just have a broken leg, but Doc will fix him up. Stop worrying for now about him. No sign of Annie yet. But we're still looking. You're going to get a fast and smoother ride on board this shiny red helicopter landing in about two minutes. They're going to take good care of you. I won't be far behind. See you at the hospital."

Her hand found him on top of the sheet. "Please?"

Please what? He wasn't sure what she was asking for reassurance on, but he knew he was going to keep whatever promise she needed. "I promise all will be taken care of. And I will see you at the hospital. You're in good hands." He stepped back and there was a strange sense of reluctance as his hand left hers. It was odd. But things often were at the scene of such accidents. At least that's what his brain was trying to get him to believe.

Three minutes later, the craft was lifting upwards and away from the site. Quiet settled. It was eerie and he didn't care for that. He had an injured dog to get help for, a scared child to calm down and reassure, and a wayward kitten who had put it all into motion. Just another day for the sheriff of Brock County.

Chapter Four

MATT MADE A quick trip to the local veterinary's office just a couple blocks from the hospital. A vet tech came out the door, obviously keeping an eye out for his arrival. A woman came behind him. Matt had the presence of mind on the way into town to call his eldest sister to meet him at the vet's and take Jillie with her until he could get off work and pick her up. She was the closest person to the situation, having her office at the courthouse and close by the hospital. And being mayor of Destiny's River, she could amend her schedule as needed. She was certainly needed in that moment.

Jillie eagerly went into the hug her aunt offered her. "And who is the furball you have in your arms? Was it in the accident also?"

"I think Jillie can explain that to you later, but no, the kitten was not exactly in the accident. The dog was. And I do appreciate you being able to lend a hand here. I'll be along to pick up Jillie as soon as we can sort some things out with the person involved. I must get to the hospital and, hopefully, begin to do that."

Tori nodded. "No problem. You know when we have dinner so try to make that if you can. Otherwise, don't worry. We'll be just fine. Do what you need to do."

Matt returned her hug and watched the pair get into Tori's car. He returned his daughter's tentative wave as they pulled away. Jillie had a huge heart, and this would take some time and talking it out for her to let go of the guilt she had voiced more than once on the way into town. But she was in a good place with the one person who had a great deal of experience over the years not only with soothing the agonies of his growing-up years, but also those of his other brother and sister. Tori was the big sister who had stepped in to be the parent to all of them as they survived the foster system and then went out into the world where she still mothered them today.

When he entered the office, the vet tech motioned for him to follow him into the back where Doc Adams and a couple of his techs were examining the dog's X-rays on the light box over the table. Matt moved up to watch but kept out of the way.

"This is one lucky little guy. A tough one for his many years. We have some bruising on his side and his left leg has a break that we will set. He'll manage with some pain meds and he's also a bit dehydrated so we'll give him an IV to help build him up a bit. But we shall see how he progresses in the next few days. Is his owner around to sign some releases?"

"I believe she was the driver and is in the emergency room at the hospital as we speak. But I'll fill her in when she has a clear head, and I'll get whatever you need."

"Sounds good." The vet nodded. "We'll hope for the best for the human patient, too."

Matt parked a few minutes later in the reserved spot close to the emergency room. He entered through the double doors and bypassed the waiting room. One of the nurses behind the desk looked up and smiled. "Good evening, Sheriff Parker. Are you looking for our latest patient?"

"I am. If she's from New York City and is named Ally Jones."

"She's in room two. They had X-rays and will soon go for a C-scan. Dr. Andrews is the on-call."

"Thanks, Miranda," he said with a nod. "I'll stick my head in and see if the doctor has a moment." He walked to the second closed door and slowly pushed it open and stepped through.

He was reminded how much he didn't like hospitals and emergency rooms. He was grateful for what they could do, but they also had memories that were and always would be tainted with the sadness of losing his wife, even after a decade had passed. In fact, it was in this same hospital. He shut the door on the memory trying to escape.

"Hello, Sheriff, I'll be right with you. We're about to send Ms. Jones off to have some more X-rays." The doctor spoke the words after a brief glance over at him, then returned to the patient.

"Is that the sheriff?" The voice was weaker than he remembered. Shouldn't she sound better? Was she worse? He stepped closer and his gaze found hers. "How's Teddy? And the little girl?"

She had been concerned for others from the moment he had found her in the car. "Teddy is in good hands. Doc Adams has x-rayed and set his leg which, besides some bruises and being unused to his new surroundings, is his major takeaway from the accident. You don't need to worry about him. I'll check in on him until you're able to do so yourself. As for the little girl, her name is Jillie, and she's my little girl. A frightened kitten she had just rescued a few minutes earlier, got loose and darted across the road. Without thought, though she certainly knows better most of the time, she ran after him just as you appeared over that rise. Everything else happened in seconds. I'm sorry all of this had to happen. But we'll do our best to make it up to you. Can you tell me where you were headed?"

She squeezed her eyes shut for a moment as she attempted to follow what he was saying. "Destiny's River. I have to get to Destiny's River."

"Well, welcome. You made it. Not exactly how you might have planned your arrival, but you are here. Who can we call you? You have family or friends here in this area who are expecting you?"

"No…there's no one I was coming to see. A friend told me all about this place and I just wanted to see it for myself."

"I see." Maybe not so much in that moment, but she had guts. "Anyone back in New York City we can call for you?"

"No. That is, there are a couple of friends, one of them I'll get in touch with when I can find my phone. Could it be in the car? And how bad is my car?"

"It was towed to a local garage here. They're very reputable. And they'll make a full report on it, but you just need to worry about getting on your feet. I'll get your phone call to you as soon as possible. But I know the doctor said you would be staying at least overnight here. They'll make sure you get what you need."

"Thank you. I don't want to be a bother to anyone.

You've been very helpful. And please, tell your little girl that I'm glad her kitten is okay and that she is too."

Her genuine words touched something. He had heard the usual comments along the way that people from the big city of New York were full of themselves, often. But maybe they just hadn't met Ally Jones. She seemed to be an exception. He stood from the chair beside the bed that he had pulled up to speak to her.

"You have to go." The words began as a question and ended up a statement midway. Was that a blush on her pale cheeks? Matt had only seen a woman blush once or twice in his life. "Of course, you're a very busy person. Thank you for being so kind to a stranger who just barged into your life." Her attempt at humor was as weak as she appeared.

"You'll find there are a lot of kind people in Destiny's River, while you're here. And I'll check on you later. Teddy is in good hands and so are you. Get some rest." He smiled and touched a finger to the brim of his hat. He thought that better than allowing his fingers to touch her hand in goodbye as they were tempted to do. He was aware of the interesting looks the nurse had given in his direction as he spoke to the patient. He nodded to the nurse as he moved toward the door. "Have a good afternoon, Jenny. Tell your husband howdy for me."

"Bye yourself, Sheriff. I'll tell him."

☆

ALLY WINCED AS the nurse and her assistant settled her into the room where she would spend the next day or two. All she needed was to get out of the hospital and get Teddy and hopefully find that Annie's box was intact. How could a trip go so wrong? And how was she going to pay for all the things that she needed to take care of? But her head hurt, and they kept giving her meds that only made her drowsy and unable to think anything through. And despite what the sheriff had said, she doubted that there were people all that friendly or trusting to total strangers. Even though he had been helpful and kind in a surprising way, he was still doing his job. The fact that his own daughter had been involved in the accident also offered another reason for him to be solicitous.

Her brain wasn't so muddled that she didn't realize that it was all an accident—no one was at fault. It could have been so much worse. What if she had hit the child? She didn't even want to allow those thoughts to remain in her head. But still, she had to worry about Teddy. Vets were expensive. Fixing cars…if it could be fixed, was going to be costly. And what about the hospital? She had no job any longer and no medical insurance. She needed to contact Mr. Jacobs to find out the status of the sale of the apartment and if the car had any insurance on it also. All of it was too much. But she knew that she had to get out of the bed and find her belongings. Then she needed to take one step at a time. She squeezed her eyes shut as the others left her alone at last. Tears seeped out beneath the lashes that came to rest on her cheeks, along with an exhausted sigh through slightly parted lips. Darkness was her refuge.

☆

"WE CERTAINLY HAVE become popular. Can't remember the last time a patient here demanded so much of our sheriff's personal time," the nurse on duty said as the familiar figure came down the hall.

He kept his smile noncommittal. "Just doing follow-up so we can close out the accident report." He didn't stop to chat but kept moving to the door of Ally's room. Matt's tall figure moved with quiet steps into the room where late afternoon shadows were peeping around the drawn slats of blinds at the windows. He stood in silence and the glistening dampness on the woman's cheeks did not miss his gaze. She had been through a lot. And she probably felt more than a little lost in a strange place. The sheriff placed the purse and the phone with its charged battery next to her bed, after he thought to switch it to silence in order to not disturb her sleep. The rest of her suitcases and bags were stacked for safekeeping in a storage room at his office. And as soon as he left the hospital, he would check on the little dog as he had promised her he would.

Matt Parker was a man of his word. But for some reason, he wanted to make certain that this stranger in their midst knew that was the case. She seemed vulnerable and alone. Nothing she had said brought that information, not in so many words, but it was just a feeling he had as he looked at how small she seemed in that hospital bed, a bruise beginning to show around the bandage that protected the cut on her forehead. What was her story? Were the tears for her own situation or for someone or something else? He was a fixer. His sister had told him that often enough. He saw a problem; he wanted to solve it. He saw someone in pain; he wanted to make it better.

And for his life, he had no idea why he acted on a sudden urge to bend down and place a featherlight kiss beside the bruise. Perhaps it was the effects of the day? Seeing Jillie in danger? Watching another human suffer through what could have been a much worse auto accident? He opted for the stress of the day. He just wasn't his usual official self. And he knew better than to push the reasoning past that. Without a backward glance, he left the room as quietly as he had entered.

Chapter Five

"ARE YOU SURE the little dog is going to be okay?"

If Matt had answered that question once since he arrived at his sister's home, he would have repeated his answer a half dozen times. "Jilliebean, the dog has a broken leg, but Doc Adams did a great job, and he expects the animal to be fine once he mends. But what we need to talk about is what happened today before the dog got hurt."

"Is the lady real mad at me? I didn't want anyone to get hurt. I thought Pumpkin would get hit by a car if he ran into the road. I didn't see a car and then when I did, it was at the same time Pumpkin ran off to the side of the road and then the car went into the ditch and all. I'm really, really sorry, Dad."

"First of all, the lady has a name…Ally Jones. And she has a mild concussion and some bruises and cuts. But she should be okay in a few days. So, it could have all been a lot worse, beginning with you. If she hadn't swerved when she did, then you would have been seriously hurt…if not worse. But she did her best to avoid you. Instead, she went into that ditch. Her car is a mess. Her dog is at the vet's after surgery on its leg. And you took ten years off my life."

"And don't forget to mention the many more gray hairs there are now, either," his sister added as she sat the glass of milk on the table in front of Jillie. She grinned at her brother who answered with a frown.

"As I was saying, action and reaction, both have their consequences. Everyone survived…this time. And she knows you are sorry. And she was worried about you and even that kitten. And why does it have a name now? I thought we agreed you were finding it a home. And not ours." He eyed his daughter who was intent on the food on her plate.

"Is that not the deal we made?" Matt was persistent when he felt there was something else going on to be dealt with.

"Yes, but he's so scared after what happened and all, Dad." She looked up with that combination of sadness yet hopefulness in those huge eyes that she could use as one of her greatest bargaining chips where he was concerned. "And I did call my friends, and their parents all said no. So, he's an orphan and everyone needs a safe place to call home, you always say that. Well, a poor lost kitten is the same, isn't it?"

"I think we have the makings of another persuasive politician in the family. She's a chip off the block of her favorite aunt."

"And on that note," Matt said, standing up from the table. "It's time to get home and get ready for another day of school. Get your backpack, Jilliebean."

"And you should check the calendar, brother dear," his sister interjected. "This is Friday. Please don't drop your daughter off at school tomorrow. Because I won't be here to pick her up. We have a cattle auction tomorrow. And we're also going to have to plan for things when this little one decides to make its arrival into this family." She highlighted her words by a caressing rub over the extended belly of a pregnant woman in her last trimester.

Matt shook his head. "It's been a long day so thanks for the reminder…both. And yes, I am working on after-school care for Jillie."

"I told you that I can walk to the library and stay there until it's time for you to pick me up," Jillie responded. "I'm a big girl, Dad. Not a child."

He gave her a long look…in silence. She tugged on the straps of the backpack and kissed her aunt's cheek. "He just treats me like a baby."

Tori patted the arm around her shoulders in commiseration with her niece, but the smile was sent to her brother. "I have news for you, my sweet girl, you will be a child to your father until you are a grandmother yourself and then some."

"Can we stop by the hospital?" Jillie spoke up a few minutes later as they passed the courthouse and waited at the red light to make the left turn toward their house on the edge of town.

"Hospital? Are you ill?" Matt cast a quick glance at his daughter.

"No, I'm not. I just think it would be a good thing to check on Miss Jones—and I could also apologize to her."

"That is an admirable thought, my daughter. But I'm sure she needs her rest so she can hurry and mend and get back on her way to wherever she's going."

"I thought I heard you tell Aunt Tori that she said she was coming here to Destiny's River for some special reason. Does she have family here or anyone she knows? She could be lonely if she doesn't."

"Forget being a politician," Matt replied. "You have a

memory for arguing a subject... Being a lawyer might be better for you. But no, we are not disturbing her this evening." He noted the crestfallen look that replaced the smile of hope from a few moments before.

"What we can do, is stop by the vet's and check on the dog. That might mean a lot to her."

Jillie's smile was huge. "That's a great idea."

"Your old dad has those once in a while."

They took a quick detour a block down and pulled up at the vet's office a few minutes later. They had late hours two days a week and this was one of those. One of the aides came out and then led the way back to where rows of cages with patients of the fur variety were visible. Some were more boisterous and vocal than others. But they were shown to an end cage that had an occupant with a bandaged leg, which had clearly been shaved of all fur, and an ugly metal pin protruded from either side of the ankle bone. The eyes were huge and melancholy as the animal lifted its small head with its protective cone in place.

"He looks so sad," Jillie whispered, bending down to see the dog better as it did not move from its place against the corner back wall. "Hello, little guy. I'm Jillie. I'm a friend."

There was a measured silence. Then a small movement of the end of its tail allowed for a brief lift before it returned to lie quietly.

"Is he okay?"

"That is the most movement the little guy has shown this afternoon," the tall, white-coated man observed walking up to join them in front of the cage. "He must like your voice, Jillie."

"Is he doing okay?" Matt looked at the man over his daughter's head and then thought better of his timing. Jillie didn't need to hear anything other than good news now that she had seen the little animal.

Doc Adams nodded with a knowing smile. "Teddy is a tough little guy. He should mend just fine after some rest and quiet. I think he's probably missing his owner and is unsure of his surroundings."

"He's lonely and afraid," Jillie said, laying a slim finger between the two bars closest to her. "Hi, Teddy. That's a nice name. I think we can be friends. I'm sorry you got hurt. I'll come visit you here until you get out. Okay?"

"He'd like that. He's been just lying there with no interest in anything until now. He's perking up having you here." The vet smiled at Jillie as the dog edged closer to allow his nose to touch the soft stroking of her finger between the bars.

Matt noted the beaming smile on his daughter's face. His daughter had had a way with animals even at an earlier age. And that often caused him to be the mean dad who would draw the line with a never-ending stream of animals of one sort or another coming through their front door with her pleading gaze and then tears when he had to put his foot down. Such as the three-legged goat that had followed her home according to her story, or the possum who made itself at home on the back porch...along with her help of a box with his old shirts adorning the inside as bedding for the animal. Luckily, both creatures had moved on to better homes...one at a petting zoo and another to a sanctuary in the next county for wild animals.

He was grateful that this dog had an owner and a place to go home after release. Or did he? That question popped up in his brain. Jillie could also have a future as a mind reader.

"And if he needs a place to stay until his owner gets better, he can stay with us, can't he, Dad?"

"Well, let's hope that doesn't happen. Don't go getting ahead of yourself, Jillie."

"May I come visit tomorrow?" Jillie turned that doe-eyed look on the vet next and Matt felt relief.

"That would be fine." The vet grinned.

"Let's let the doctor get home and we need to do the same. Say good night to your friend."

"Good night, Teddy. I'll be here tomorrow to visit again. You be good and hurry and get well."

The sun had set, and the town square had quieted. There were the usual patrons parked at the downtown eateries: the café and the pizzeria. And farther down, the parking lot in front of the local cinema was filling up. Other cars were heading out to the restaurant and dance hall along the river for nicer dining and then dancing after. Or there were those who headed in the opposite direction to the bowling and arcade building on the opposite side of downtown. Destiny's River was settling into the early autumn evening. A few weeks until Thanksgiving and then the Christmas festivities would take over.

Matt had to admit that he felt a pride inside to be part of such a beautiful small town nestled at the entrance to the Hill Country region of Texas, with its tall hills, ice-cold clear spring-fed rivers and lakes, and deep canyons and tranquil grass-covered meadows. The people were an added plus. They welcomed strangers and made them feel part of the town, no matter where they came from. He was forever grateful that his eldest sister had set out to find a place for them all to call home many years ago as they all aged out of the foster system. She had a dream to find such a place and she didn't rest until she had made it come true. Three of the four Parker siblings had made their way to call Destiny's River home. The hope was that, eventually, the final sibling—his brother—would leave his rambling ways behind and make it unanimous. Until then, he would do his part as sheriff of the county to see that such a good community maintained what made it special.

They arrived home and Jillie hurried ahead of him to make sure the new kitten, Pumpkin, was still in its sleeping box in the utility room. The moment the kitten saw her, its meows began, and naturally, Jillie had to pick it up and cradle it.

"Jillie..." Matt began but his daughter was ahead of him.

"I know, Dad. But he's still getting used to things and I'll calm him down and then bring him back to his box. He's just a scared baby." And the child and kitten cradled in her arms were disappearing up the stairs to her room before Matt uttered another word.

And another battle lost even before he'd said a word. Matt shook his head. His sister had been right when she mentioned the gray hairs he kept finding. And ninety percent were the result of being the father of a daughter like Jillie. He had to admit it was times like these and others that he missed not having the support in the house of another sane adult. It was times he wished he might find someone who would be the mother figure that his daughter deserved. But no such person had crossed his path to date. Maybe he was being too picky? That had been mentioned a time or two or three by his two sisters. Even by his daughter. Everyone in town seemed to have placed their two cents worth on the subject over the years. He took a cold drink from the refrigerator and popped the lid. He sank down in his easy chair and settled back, replaying the long day's events.

Ally Jones. New York City, New York. She was a long way from home. But somehow, seeing a couple of the boxes that his deputy had stacked inside their storeroom waiting for her to take off their hands, he noted items one wouldn't normally find on just a vacation-type trip. Some pots and pans, a couple dishes, linens, blanket, even a pillow. He hadn't looked any further. There wasn't any real reason for him to do so. But it had stayed in his mind. And there was another box that his deputy had brought to his attention. And that had also stuck in his questioning brain. It was hand-carved, with an inlaid engraved plate on the top surrounded by carved roses. The workmanship was beautiful. It clearly held cremains. A mother? That was interesting also. One didn't usually take trips with their loved one's remains. Still, there was no law against it.

All in all, he shouldn't be giving the woman in the hospital another thought. She was the doctor's responsibility, not his. Still…there was *something*. But then his attention was caught by a movement next to his feet and his mind jumped to it. A bright-eyed bit of orange fur was looking up at him. He shook his head and called out in his loud 'parent' voice: "Jillie Anne Parker!"

Chapter Six

"JILLIE PARKER...WHAT ARE you doing here? Seeing a friend?" The nurse looked up from the screen in front of her and greeted the girl with a welcoming smile.

"Sort of," Jillie responded with a slight smile and a larger amount of nerves. "It's Miss Jones and my dad was here yesterday because she was in an accident and..."

"Miss Jones is in 326, just three doors down that hall on the right," the nurse spoke up with a nod of her head in the correct direction. "She just had her lunch so she should be awake, and you can go right on in. Those are pretty flowers you brought."

Jillian increased her grip on the stems of the flowers wrapped in their pink tissue paper and thanked the woman. She walked with steps that slowed as she got closer to the door. Taking a deep breath, she gave a tentative knock on the door. She didn't have to wait long as a soft voice called out, "Come in."

Jillian pushed open the door and stepped inside, then paused just across the threshold.

"Hello, I was expecting a nurse. Are you in the wrong room?" *Poor thing,* Ally thought as she noted the nervous smile and wide eyes. The child was expecting someone she knew to be in the room, and she must look a fright with her bruised head and bandage.

"No ma'am," the child responded with a faint voice and shake of her head. Then Ally noted that she squared her small shoulders a bit and made tentative steps closer to the bed. "My name is Jillie Parker, and I wanted to come by and bring you flowers. And I know Teddy—and I wanted to let you know that he misses you very much, but I promised him I would visit him and now you and let you know he is okay and all." She finally paused and drew in a breath.

"Well, thank you, Miss Jillie. And thank you for the pretty flowers. I like pink and you are the very first to bring me flowers. I've never had a bouquet before. And thank you so much for visiting Teddy. I was so worried about him. But how did you know to visit him or about me?"

"My dad." The voice was minus the nerves, and she warmed to the subject. "My dad let me go see Teddy and I can visit him each day until you get better. And you really never had any flowers before?" The bouquet was handed over to Ally. "Not even from a boyfriend or anyone?"

Ally shook her head and found it very easy to smile at the child. "Nope. No boyfriend or anyone. You are the first and that makes them very special. But who is your dad? A doctor?"

"No, he's the sheriff. He helped you at the wreck and all." Then the smile faded from the little girl's face. "I'm sorry. It was my fault. I was trying to keep my kitten out of the road, and he just ran across and then you were there and...I should have stayed in the car like my dad said but I just wanted to save the kitten."

"Did you save him?"

Jillie nodded. "And he's an orphan and my dad acts like he doesn't want me to keep him but I know he'll learn to like him. Dad just has to act all grown-up and stuff. But he's a softie…most of the time."

Ally couldn't help but grin at the girl's description. That wasn't the impression she had gotten upon meeting the tall, quiet man. He was all professional when handling things at the accident and ensuring she was helped and even going above and beyond with helping her Teddy and then securing her belongings. He had an aura about him that made her feel his sense of calm and that she was in a safe place and help was there for her. She would have to set aside the 'softie' comment for the time being and take his daughter's word for it.

"Do you have siblings?" It was an innocent enough question to ask in being polite to her young visitor.

"No." She shook her head, with a bit of sadness or regret tinging her tone. "I wish I did. I just have cousins. But my mother died when I was a baby and it's just my dad and me. Although there are plenty of women in town who try to get my dad's attention and make nice over me when he's around and all. Guess they think that will make him like them more or something."

"I see. I'm sorry about your mother. I lost mine when I was very young also. I had often wished for a sister or brother, too. But you are lucky you have a family with cousins in it." She knew the matter-of-fact summation of the child's family was a familiar defense mechanism. She had grown up with much the same delivery whenever anyone had questions about her past. But she had the impression also that Jillie had a different set of circumstances than those she had been raised with. She was a sweet little girl ready to step into the next stage of her life if she gauged her age correctly.

"How old are you? What grade are you in?"

"I'm almost eleven…in another six months. But my teachers say that I am mature for my age. I'm in the fifth grade."

"Not too mature, or you would have let me know where you took off to instead of going to the sweet shop like you said you were." The voice surprised them both. The softie dad didn't look too much like a softie at the moment in Ally's estimation. He had entered the room without notice and caught the last of their conversation.

"I'm sorry, Dad. But when I got to the sweet shop, I saw the flower shop across the street, and I just thought maybe some pretty ones would help brighten the hospital room and it was just another three blocks to the hospital. I did see Deputy Grover on the street corner and asked him to let you know where I was headed. I was going to hurry right back. But…"

"But it's my fault," Ally spoke up. "I kept her longer by just visiting with her. I'm sorry if you were worried."

The man removed his cowboy hat and swept a hand through the hair at his forehead. He had nice thick hair of a chestnut color, a bit longish compared to the short cuts she was used to seeing on police in the city. And his tan jeans fit a toned length of leg that indicated, along with a broad chest in a crisp white, long-sleeved shirt, that he probably worked out on a regular basis. She had to smile when she saw the polished black boots. Cowboy hat and cowboy boots…a

Texas lawman. He even had a gun holstered at his hip and a bright shiny silver badge to go with it all. *Nice.* But those green eyes were locked on hers when she realized she had been taking a silent inventory of the man, and she felt a warmth rise in her cheeks. For the first time, she realized that she probably looked quite a sight herself but not in a complimentary way. She had little makeup, her hair needed good shampooing, and the gray hospital gown did nothing for her paleness. Not her best foot forward.

"I was worried. But Jillie and I will discuss that at home. I hope she hasn't disturbed you too much." His voice had a deep tone that she remembered from the accident. It was very pleasant.

"She's a breath of fresh air in this hospital room. And the flowers are the most wonderful surprise. I do appreciate what she…what you both have done and are doing, including taking your time to check on a stranger's dog. It seems some of the things I've been told over the years about this small town called Destiny's River are indeed not exaggerations. The friendliness of everyone I've met so far is incredible."

"That reminds me," he said, stepping forward and raising the glass vase he had in his other hand. "The nurse asked me to bring this in to you. She thought it might come in handy when she saw the flowers in my daughter's hands."

"Thank you," Ally said, indicating a spot on the table next to her. "I'll get the nurse to put them in water for me."

Jillie spoke up. "I can do that for you." She took the vase from her dad. "Aren't people friendly where you come from?" It was an innocent question from Jillie.

"Well…" Ally took some time to consider her response

"...they can be for the most part, but in a different way. They're a bit more reserved and take longer to warm up to someone. Guess they're more wary in a way. But it is such a huge place, and it really is a city that never sleeps. There is noise and activity around the clock. It can be overwhelming to someone coming into it brand new and not knowing what to expect."

"Were you able to make contact with your friend in New York?" It sounded like a natural question from the sheriff, and Ally took it as such.

She nodded. "Mr. Jacobs is an attorney and executor of my friend's estate. He's also been a good friend to us both over the years. He's sending me copies of the insurance policy and all other information on the car. And he was helpful with other things about this trip." She stopped there. Jillie's surprising arrival had come just as she had completed her conversation with the man. She hadn't had time to wrap her head around some of the information he had provided on the status of the sale of the apartment. But she would tackle that problem once her visitors had left.

Jillie had completed the task of putting water in the vase and arranging the flowers inside it. She sat the floral display on the table beside Ally's bed. They brightened the plain room.

"We've taken up enough of Miss Jones's quiet time. She needs her rest so she can mend and get out of here...the hospital, I mean. We hope you'll be able to spend some time in our town. It may be smaller than you're used to, but there are quiet charms to be found and good people. I'll check on your vehicle if you like and see if D and J have come up with an idea of the damages and repairs needed."

Ally nodded. "I'm afraid that I'm clueless when it comes to automobiles and certainly anything wrong with them. If you could check with the mechanics and then give me their address and contact information, I'd appreciate it. I'll need to speak to them as soon as possible. I'm stranded until my vehicle is situated and hopefully in working condition."

"That's not a problem. I'll be glad to stop by there and check on it. I'll be in touch after I do. Let's let this lady rest now, Jillie." He slid his hat over his head and held the door for his daughter to join him.

"I'll tell Teddy about the visit with you when I see him this afternoon. He'll be happy—I know it." Jillie grinned at Ally, and she returned it.

"Thank you, Jillie. Both of you, for all your kindnesses."

The door whispered shut behind the pair.

It didn't stay shut for long. The nurse who had introduced herself as Taylor when she had begun the morning shift earlier came breezing through the door with a couple of med cups in her hand. "Sorry, sorry…meant to get here sooner with your meds, but we had two more admits to this floor." She was all smiles as she handed the meds to Ally and then the cup of water sitting next to her bed.

"Thank you so much," Ally said. "Do you know Jillie and her family?"

"In this town, everyone knows everyone. Guess it's a lot different where you come from, right?" She made note on the computer across from the bed of the meds administered and any notes she deemed necessary. "I can't imagine living in such a huge place as New York City. I would get lost the moment I stepped off the plane. I don't even like going to Dallas and it's real big too."

Ally smiled. "Well, it takes some getting used to, but once you figure out how to get around...mostly on foot or subway...you can map out your own routine."

"Well, in answer to your first question, yes, I and my family know Jillie and the Parkers and the Lockwood's and..."

"Lockwood?" Ally heard a familiar name...or at least one she recognized from reading it in the note left for her by Annie. She had finally read the note handed to her by the attorney as she was about to leave New York. But the instructions had been clear: *read only when you arrive in Destiny's River*. Well, it had been before dawn and before others began stirring in the hospital when she had finally opened it. And that name was in the note.

Taylor moved over to stand next to the bed. "Yes, the Lockwood's were one of the founding families of Destiny's River from way back when. Caden Lockwood, the family member in charge now, married Tori, the oldest sister of Sheriff Parker and Jillie's aunt. She is a nice person. She moved here and bought the Primrose Inn, a beautiful old Victorian place, and then she became our first lady mayor, and she keeps getting reelected. Her meeting Caden Lockwood was a real romance story. And now they're expecting their baby soon."

"You said she was the oldest sister? He has more in the family?" She wasn't prying so much as trying to see where everyone fit together in Annie's story.

"Yes, there is Cassie who came to protect another ranching family over in Red Bluffs from this drug lord, and then she fell in love with the rancher, and they got married after the case was over. Cassie is Matt's younger sister. And then there's Rance—he's a U.S. Marshal and is single, too. Seems it's a tad bit hard to rope in those Parker boys but believe me the females line up to try."

"I see. And they all live here in this town?"

"Matt and his oldest sister do, of course. Cassie's just a few miles away on their ranch. And Rance, well he comes home rarely except holidays or weddings." Taylor laughed. "He is always on some case and lives down south of Austin way for his job."

"Sounds like quite a family. It's nice to have such closeness and roots…I would imagine."

"It is—mine is the same way. But you can get tired of each other now and then." She laughed once again. "But it is pretty good to know they are there no matter what when it counts."

"I can imagine." Ally paused. "Will the doctor be by later today?"

"Yes, he'll make his rounds once he's done with surgery. You sound like you're in a hurry to leave our fine hotel here."

"It is indeed fine, and everyone has been so kind and caring. But I need to get on my feet and see if I have a car that still runs and see if my dog remembers me," she said, trying to make light of what brought her to the hospital in the first place. She had a lot of things to get done and no idea how she would do them all, but she needed to figure it out.

"I LIKE MISS Jones," Jillie pronounced as they pulled into the parking lot of the café. "She's nice. Don't you think so?"

Matt turned off the engine then gave a considering look at his daughter. "I suppose she is nice…especially considering all she's been through the last couple of days."

They entered the café, which was filling up for the early afternoon weekend lunch crowd…residents combined with out-of-towners driving out from the cities to search for treasures in the small-town shops and enjoy the many wineries that had sprung up in the Hill Country. Tori waved at them from a corner table. They were soon seated with her, and Wallace, her assistant.

"Where's Cade and the rest of your crew?" Matt asked, accepting the iced tea sat in front of him by the smiling waitress.

"I took the liberty already of ordering your iced tea and your soft drink, Jilliebean," Tori said. "Food is up to you. We ordered the enchilada plate."

"No need to look at menus." Matt nodded at the waitress. "We always come on weekend lunch for those homemade enchiladas of Maggie's." Jillie nodded in agreement.

"So, what have you two been up to?" Tori asked, taking a sip of her tea but with her gaze on Matt.

"Why do I think you know the answer to that question already by that look you're giving me?" Matt was a seasoned veteran of his sister's ploys.

"Well, since you said that, I will tell you that it's been the talk of the café here until you walked in the door. So, I just had to keep my ears open."

"We were at the hospital," Jillie chimed in. "I took her flowers and then Dad came because I didn't let him know I was doing that."

"Really? Well, the way I heard it, *Dad* took our new visitor in town some flowers today after visiting her yesterday, too. People found it interesting that our sheriff never did that with anyone else around here. But they didn't mention that he took his daughter along. Silly gossips."

"Yes indeed." Matt nodded. "Silly people with nothing better to do with their time—and they certainly don't bother to get facts straight before spreading the manure."

"Matthew! Watch your language around big ears at this table." Tori grinned while trying to maintain a stern look and failing with a wink at Jillie. Jillie had to laugh at that point.

"Manure isn't a bad word, Aunt Tori. Dad says it a lot when he doesn't want to say those other words around me."

"And it isn't a topic of conversation over food, so change the subject." He was glad the plate of food made it to the table at that juncture. Once all of them had their food, he concentrated on eating and hoped the topic would change.

He had hoped in vain. "So, what are our visitor's plans when she's released? I hear her vehicle is in need of some serious repair. That might mean she's stranded here for a while."

"Well thanks for that update," Matt said not bothering to look up at his sister. "I won't need to go by Dee's and get an update."

"Dad told Ally he would do that and tell her more when he goes back to see her later." And thanks to his daughter for chiming in and making matters worse.

"Going back again? My, she is certainly a popular patient. I might have to drop by and say hi when I see my obstetrician for my checkup later. Just be the neighborly thing to do."

Matt looked at her then with a silent brother to nosy sister message in his gaze. "I don't see any need in that. A patient is to rest in the hospital, not have a social calendar."

"Well, I'm practically family to her given the gossip this morning. So, I should do the neighborly thing."

"Can I go with you, Aunt Tori? I want to tell her about Teddy."

"Teddy? Who is he?"

"Her dog. He was hurt in the accident and Doc Adams is taking good care of him. I told her that I was visiting him for her while she's in the hospital."

"I see." And Matt knew that tone. "Jillie, why don't you go look in the dessert case over there and see what kind of pies they have there today?"

"Okay," she said, standing up, but then she turned with a wink at him, "but I know you don't really want to know that—you just want to speak with Aunt Tori, and you don't want me to hear. But I'll go."

His sister couldn't help the laugh as she watched the girl cross the room. "Nice try, brother. She's not a child any longer."

"Neither are you, but you act like one sometimes. Drop this gossip thing."

"Wise up, brother of mine. Let your sister give you some sage advice. Here is a perfect opportunity to get the single females off your trail...for a little while at least."

"I know I shouldn't ask...but what is in that peabrain of yours now?"

"It's quite simple. The best way to put a chill on the local ladies is to present them with a *fait accompli*...in simpler terms for you...the girl of your dreams. A fake girlfriend...even better a fake fiancée. Someone they know nothing about but are already jealous of since she's claimed your attention since she arrived...so to speak. Love at first sight. They're already trying to find out when she's leaving. And since it sounds like between her car and her dog...she just might be around for a couple weeks or so if we're lucky...that will cool their interest in you. Give you a breather. And there is more."

"I don't think I can take more of that brain of yours. Have you thought about getting it checked?"

"The more is that she can stay at Primrose. The Morrisons are going to Italy to visit their daughter and her husband and to be there for the birth of their first grandchild. I need someone to stay on the property while they're gone. Beautiful, quiet place to recuperate and, it comes with a salary for her time. That might come in handy to help ease her concerns about those hospital bills and car repairs in addition to having a place to stay and all. It's a win-win for your entire family and for her. My genius surprises even me sometimes."

"That would be great! Teddy can stay and I can visit him and..." Jillie had arrived and evidently caught part of her crazy aunt's idea. Matt set his fork down.

"Thought you were looking at the pie selection?"

"I can't stand there for hours while you two talk grown-up stuff. So, I had to come back to the table. But I think it's a super plan." She sat back down in her chair with a huge smile.

"Well, there is one saving grace in all of this," he conceded, "and that is she seems to be a smart lady and won't agree to such a scheme. Now, what were the pie selections?"

"Chocolate, strawberry, coconut cream, apple," she recited. "But what about..."

"Now, now, Jilliebean..." her aunt spoke up, patting her hand that lay on the table "...your father has spoken. We need to let him eat his dessert in peace. I think I'll have apple." She smiled at her niece. Then signaled their waitress.

Matt breathed a sigh of relief. But then he caught the sideward glance his sister gave his daughter. Was that a quick wink? Surely, not. But then...that sinking feeling came over him when he remembered how easily she had given up. His sister never gave up that easily. There was danger ahead...and all one could usually do was hold on tight...and hope to survive.

Chapter Seven

"I KNOW IT sounds bad right now, Ally, but it won't be long before all will be settled," Mr. Jacobs's voice sounded positive, and he did his best to relieve her fears. But all she knew was that she was still sliding between that rock and a hard place that she often felt during her life. While she was used to things not quite turning out for the best in some circumstances, she had hoped. For the first time in a long time, she had felt hopeful that even though Annie was gone, and she and Teddy were basically homeless, it would all just be temporary. But then life had thrown one of its usual curveballs even in Destiny's River.

"If we were able to close on the sale of the apartment as we had thought, then all would have been placed in the account by now. As it is, what you were able to begin your trip on was from the estate sale of the furnishings and things. The car repairs to get it in shape for a long trip came about from the bank account and savings provided for expenses along the way and with a little leftover. But the car repairs from the accident, minus insurance, will still leave a deficit. The sooner we can get the sale closed on the apartment, the better. And we are hopeful that the buyer can close on their present property in a couple of weeks and then we can close on Annie's. When that happens, you will have more than enough funds to cover what is left and send you on your way to whatever destination you choose and have a start there. In the meantime, why don't you open an account there in Destiny's River and allow me to send you a loan on part of the amount? That way you—"

Ally shook her head as she responded: "Thank you, Mr. Jacobs, but no. You have done so much for Annie over the years and now for me in trying to do what she wanted with this trip. That is something I don't want to do. I will figure things out here until the apartment is sold. Then it will all be okay. But I do thank you so much for the offer."

"Well, you keep it in mind just in case. I'm serious. We miss you up here. The kids in the choir ask about you all the time. If you decide to come back east, then we're all here to welcome you. You just promise to call me no matter the time if you need anything. Okay?"

"I promise and give my love to all the kids. I miss them, too. I'll keep in touch."

When the call ended, an intense sadness settled over her. She felt the loneliness close in just like it had the moment she had lost Annie. Ally had no idea how to do it but she needed to find a way to make it through the next weeks on what was left in her account, which had to cover a place to stay, transportation, food, and being able to pay for Teddy's stay and hers in the hospital…neither of which she would have ever counted on having to do. But life just kept throwing the curveballs. She brushed a quick hand over her eyes just as a voice surprised her.

"I hope I'm not intruding at a bad time? I'm Matt Parker's sister, Tori, and wanted to stop by and say hello."

Ally sat up a bit straighter against her pillows and pushed down all the other emotions of the moment previous to the appearance of the woman at her door. "Please…I'm fine. Come in."

Tori moved to stand by the bed. "I know that after a while, a hospital room can get to be depressing and you want to be any place else." Her voice was soft and kind and Ally found it pushing the sadness off to the side. She summoned a better smile for her visitor.

"Please sit," she said, and motioned to the chair a foot or so away from the stand where the bouquet sat. Tori took the seat.

"Thank you. I told the nurses outside that I wouldn't stay long, but I heard my niece sing your praises at lunch earlier and thought I might stop in as I have my doctor's appointment here in the same complex."

"Is this your first baby?"

"Yes. And it is quite the experience." She laughed and Ally joined in. "But they are blessings, and we're thankful this one seems to be as healthy as possible. And how are you feeling? Are they taking good care of you?"

"Oh yes, they're all so nice and kind and I don't have any complaints."

"Good. Because as mayor, I'd have to do something about how they might be treating any visitors who happen to end up in here while in Destiny's River." They both laughed at her words.

"You are a very busy lady."

"A busy lady who will be taking a bit of time off from my other duties to concentrate on this new bundle of joy.

I'm really sorry that this happened to you, but I also am not in another way."

Ally must have looked confused at those last few words. Tori hurried to clarify.

"Well, you've met Jillie, my adorable and incredible little niece. Matt keeps busy with being the sheriff. He is a great dad… Don't get me wrong. But his time can be limited so we all try to help out each other when someone in the family needs it. I've been the one picking up Jillie after school and taking care of errands and dinner and homework stuff…all of the usual stuff that's necessary with a child in school and a parent who works long hours sometimes."

"I imagine you're considered quite a godsend for those things you do to help them."

"Well, I hope so, but I've been worrying about that. I won't be able to do those things for a few weeks after the baby comes, which could be in the next two to three weeks. That leaves Matt in a bind. I've been trying to find someone who would suit the bill, but it isn't as easy as it might seem here in Destiny's River. Many are too old or not patient enough to take care of the running around involved—and then some are too young…and too single. If you get my drift."

"Too single?"

"I'm pretty straightforward and will just get to the point, okay?"

Ally nodded. "Please do. I prefer to be that way myself."

"I sensed that about you. And my senses are seldom off." She grinned. "So, here's the deal. My brother lost his dear wife right after Jillie was born. He has shouldered the raising of his daughter and taking care of a high-pressure job and done it all without fault and without any complaint. People respect him and love him in these parts."

"I think I hear a loud *but* coming," Ally commented.

"*But*...the women in these parts, the single ones...have zeroed in on him and it seems to just get worse. It really does upset him these days. Before, he could shrug it off and even laugh about it a time or two, but it has gotten out of hand. Anyway...back to the problem at hand. It seems you will need a place to stay. You might not have counted on needing to stay a while, but because of the accident that may have changed things for you. And you are recuperating and so is your little dog—which Jillie told me about. Well...I have a beautiful home here in town. The couple who were caretaking for me have gone to Italy for six weeks to be with their only daughter who is about to have her first baby. Her husband is stationed over there. Anyway, I just need someone to stay in the house...rent-free.

"And if that person could also be available in the afternoons to pick up Jillie and help with errands and dinners sometimes when Matt might run late, that would be such a huge help and a load off my mind. There's a car that you would have free use of also. It's really a good deal for all of us when you think of it. And besides, in six or seven weeks, you might just decide that you want to stay even longer in our town. It's a great place to put down roots. I know that from firsthand knowledge. I came here looking for a home for me and my siblings, and I found it. And I found the love of my life at the same time."

"Wow. I can only think of that word. Are you a mind

reader by any chance?" Ally was amazed. A few minutes ago, her world had just about imploded. Then a woman walks in and hands her the answer to most, if not all, of her prayers. Annie's words came back to her at the same time. She had been telling Ally about her life back in Destiny's River and she could still see her face as she spoke about it. *"Mark my words, Ally girl...when you find your place in the world, I hope it's a lot like Destiny's River. There is peace like no other, knowing you belong to it, and it belongs to you. Your heart will let you know that."*

"I must admit that this would be of great help and would give me peace of mind knowing that I would have time to get my vehicle and my dog and even myself back on track again...and take care of many worries. Jillie seems like a delightful little girl and that would be a very easy task to help her and her dad...and you, as well. Your family has certainly been so kind and helpful. I would like to return that in some way."

"Then that is wonderful for all of us! Isn't it amazing when help comes when you least expect it? But living here in Destiny's River...it isn't that surprising. Stick around and you'll see more of what I'm talking about. So when the doctor releases you, we'll get you all settled into Primrose Inn. And even though it has 'inn' in the name, I haven't taken in guests in a few years. It's just become a very special place for our families and those we care about. You'll see what I mean. It's a wonderful place."

"I can just imagine. I'll be glad to help in any way that I can." Ally's heart felt lighter than it had in many months. "It is indeed an unexpected answer to many needs."

Tori stood and nodded. "Yes, it is that. And I'll check in later for any updates on your release. In the meantime, we'll be getting Primrose Inn ready for its next guest. Do get your rest, and hopefully it will be peaceful now."

Ally closed her eyes and leaned back into the pillows, taking a long breath and exhaling it. She replayed the whole of Tori's visit several times. Each time it ended with her disbelief that such an answer to her problems had materialized all at once and when least expected.

She wasn't quite sure why the woman had begun speaking of her brother, and the loss of his wife, and where things stood in the community as far as his marriage eligibility. Maybe she was just bolstering her argument in the belief of how it might help the family's stress levels…given the timing of things. At any rate, she wasn't going to fixate the advent of the offer. It would allow her to get her life back under control after the accident and the complications it brought to her life and the plan. She would be able to regain her momentum and to follow through on Annie's last wishes. The money she would save on lodging would be an answer to a prayer itself and along with the salary for helping with Jillie's care…that should tide all of it over until the sale of the apartment and funds would be available for her to move on with her life. What that life would look like, she had no idea, but possibilities were always just around the corner as Annie would often say. She would hold on to that thought.

☆

"YOU DID WHAT?" Matt's office door was closed, and he was

glad of it. The sheriff raising his voice to the mayor might not play well among those on the first floor of the courthouse.

"Calm down, Matthew," she responded, settling back in the chair across from his, placing a wide expanse of oak desk between them. "Sit down and take a breath. You really should be careful of your blood pressure. You aren't getting any younger."

"Cut the blood pressure BS and explain why in the blue blazes you would think of such a scheme. You don't really know anything about this person. And you decided that she would be good to take over after-school care for Jillie?"

"Do you seriously think I don't know the answers to my questions before I ask them? I do my homework. You should try it sometime. But Ally was kind enough to offer up a contact that I could call…in fact three…but it only took me one to learn more about her than I wager you have. I am comfortable with having her stay in Primrose Inn, and more than secure in the fact that her experience with children in the choir at her church in New York and childcare settings will be just what we both need for peace of mind—and Jillie certainly already likes her. Besides, she'll keep the wolves at bay from your doorstep. What do you call it when all roads come together and make a grand intersection of chance? Perfection?"

"More like the Bermuda Triangle."

Tori shook her head and stood. "Honestly, little brother, sometimes I marvel that we're related. You can be so obstinate and shortsighted."

Matt stood also. "I marvel at it, too. But I call it being

thorough and clear-minded. You might take lessons. And to remind you, I am the sheriff. I have a lot of access to information that most do not. To think that I have not already done a deep dive into our visitor shows how little you should assume you know. That was done before the sun rose on her second day here."

"I did knock but Deputy Grover said I might want to borrow a SWAT helmet. Your voices were raised a bit, so I waited a couple of minutes." Caden Lockwood, Tori's husband, peeked around the doorway with a grin on his face.

"Please come in," Matt invited with a sweep of his hand, "but only if you plan to take your wife someplace else."

"Very amusing." Tori made a grimace at her brother but stood on tiptoe to plant a kiss on her husband's cheek. "I would say maybe you can talk some sense into him, but that requires him to have a brain. Let's go, dear." She gave a tug on his arm and he had just enough time to shoot a look of commiseration in Matt's direction. "I'll take one for the team. Have a good afternoon." The pair shut the door behind them.

Matt launched the pencil still in his hand onto the far corner of his desk and slumped back into the chair's seat. He spun around to fix his gaze out the window where it was a perfect fall afternoon, with sunshine and trees turning leaves into muted greens, burnt oranges, and pale yellows. But he wasn't really enjoying it. His brain was going over the half-baked idea his sister had just lobbed like a grenade into the peace of his office.

Yes, they needed someone for after-school duties to help with Jillian while Tori was out with a new baby. And yes, the pickings were turning up slim in the small town. Either too old, too young, or too single. Even some of the married ones had been marked off the list due to more interest in the dad than the daughter. But Tori had overstepped. It should have been him who found a suitable answer and set things in motion. But Tori had, as usual, gone right ahead and organized everyone's life and then let him in on it. But just because he didn't plow ahead like a bull in a china closet, did not mean he wasn't doing due diligence. He preferred to do things quietly and his way. He was looking at both sides of the situation and the answers were swirling in his brain. When he was ready to make his decision known, he would.

Was she wrong? His brain wasn't quick to answer that one. And that might be what irritated him the most. Looking at it all objectively, without being so closely involved as he was, he might have jumped on the bandwagon and checked off the list and marked it done. So, what was stopping him? He was just irritable. Why? The usual job issues? Nothing new there. Something amiss about the new visitor or her arrival? Well, he couldn't really put any blame on her when it was his daughter's fault, and Ally Jones hadn't planned to have an accident and be stranded for any amount of time in Destiny's River. So, what was the issue?

Think positives and not negatives. Sage advice he had used over the years from being raised in the foster care system with his siblings, to trying to raise a child on his own, and keeping a whole county safe at the same time. Positives about Ally Jones? She was nice. She had responded with warmth and kindness with Jillie. He hadn't seen a moment of feeling sorry for herself but rather concern for others…including her dog. He had been pleased by what Tori had mentioned about her involvement with children back in New York. She had a heart for kids and animals. And even his interfering sister. She would have wanted to help a woman expecting a child—that was something he would bet on. A person's soul could be glimpsed in their eyes. And there was a time or two he had been drawn to them. But it was from concern. And why did that seem to be something he was trying to convince himself of? *Strange.*

But his sister was going too far by suggesting that the female sharks in the town would be put off by Ally's appearance in their lives. When sharks smelled fresh blood, they circled closer. Waiting for the moment to strike. Ally Jones was not bait. And he wasn't about to let anyone harm her. And with that thought he envisioned his sister and knew she had done it again. Drew him in just like any other unsuspecting fly to her web.

Chapter Eight

"WELL, YOU HIT the jackpot. You must have been born under a lucky star," the nurse said, breezing through the doorway with a folder of papers in her hand, allowing the door to close behind her.

Ally paused in brushing her hair, trying to get some order to it without the help of much of her makeup or other sundries that were in a suitcase in a storage room. "Jackpot?"

"You're being released a day sooner than first thought and that is good. Second, you get to stay at the Primrose Inn…which is just gorgeous and romantic as all get out. But the real prize is that you're being chauffeured to your new digs by none other than our hunk of a sheriff himself. In fact, he's waiting just outside at the nurses' station for you. Too bad you don't need a private duty nurse to come along and help you out, because it would be an honor to jump right in and raise my hand to volunteer."

Ally gave a knowing smile. "I'm sure it would be a hardship to volunteer and all. But I don't think it would have much to do with me. Besides, you're a happily married woman or so the nurse on duty told me last night."

"Too true. You got me there. My Roy is a pretty good guy…have him all broke in and don't have the energy to do that all over again even with someone as gorgeous as Matt

Parker." She grinned. "If you're ready, we'll go over your discharge papers and appointments for checkups in a week or so." Ally perched on the side of the bed and Taylor went over the papers and answered any questions.

There was a knock on the door. Taylor gathered the folder and walked over to open it. The sheriff stood there, his hands on the handles of a wheelchair. "I told Jimmy, the orderly, that I would take it from here. He didn't seem to mind. Hope neither of you object."

"No objection here." The nurse grinned again and looked over to Ally, who was still sitting on the edge of the bed.

"None here," Ally agreed, while wishing that she had been able to do a bit more with her appearance. The bruise was smaller but purpling even more. It didn't exactly go with the dark green pullover sweater she had arrived at the hospital wearing, coupled with the same jeans. Taylor had supplied shampoo and other toiletries so at least she'd been able to shower and look a little presentable. She bent to try to get her remaining tennis shoe on her foot but it was slow going with her head still sore. A grimace replaced the smile.

"Here, let me." The sheriff was across the room and taking the sneaker from her hand in a swift move. He went down on one knee, his hand taking control of her sock-covered foot.

"A real Prince Charming there. You've been practicing, Sheriff Parker?" Taylor was watching from the doorway, and she shot a quick wink over to Ally.

To his credit, Matt didn't look up but took care of the task at hand. Only once the shoe was on and the lace tied with a small flourish did he glance up from his kneeling position, and Ally felt the full force of a Matt Parker smile…for a couple of seconds…and then it faded behind the countenance of a sheriff who became all business again. He pushed into a standing position, turning to move the wheelchair closer to her side of the bed.

"Thank you for your help with the shoe, but I don't need for you to push me in a wheelchair. Save it for the patients in here who might need it."

"None of that," Taylor interjected, and her demeanor took on her professional stance on the subject. "Hospital policy. Get a free ride outside. Enjoy it while you can." She propped the door open and then picked up the small case holding what few items Ally had in her room, along with the bouquet of flowers from Jillie's visit. The trio left the room and headed down the hallway to the elevator.

Ally couldn't help but note the glances from the staff behind the desk. Some were covert in their surveillance, while others were clearly interested in watching the patient getting personalized treatment from their prized lawman. There was one who didn't bother to mask her disapproval. Ally felt the chill in the sharp gaze sent like an arrow straight through her without any attempt to temper it. She felt an instant thanks inside that their paths had never crossed while she had been a patient. And was not likely to come across her path again.

Once outside, Taylor waited while Matt helped Ally get settled in the front seat of the large white pickup with the emblem and markings of sheriff of Brock County. The door closed and the next leg of Ally's journey was beginning. She had no idea what it would encompass but she longed for something familiar in that moment. A final wave of thanks at the nurse and the vehicle moved away from the parking lot. Ally used the time while the sheriff made a call to his office to take in the tidy little streets they made their way down. The houses were situated on lawns that were more golden in color than green now, but all were well-kept. Flower beds were evident with some greenery but obviously awaiting blooms in warmer weather. Tall trees, some with leaves and some without, were spread throughout and lined the roadway in the area that soon led to the center of what she supposed was the town of Destiny's River itself. A tall stone building sat quite imposing in the center of an expanse of grass and trees. Sidewalks led from the street on all four sides to wide steps that had people entering and exiting as they drove past. To her surprise, the vehicle slowed and pulled into a reserved space in front of the building.

Matt did not turn off the engine, but a tall, younger man in a uniform that denoted he was also a law officer was clearly coming down the sidewalk to meet them. Matt pushed a button, and his window lowered.

"Good morning, Sheriff," the younger man said to his boss and then he saw Ally, and he greeted her with a smile and a touch of two fingers to the brim of the cowboy hat he wore in a move she had seen in a few westerns that she and Annie would watch on Saturday afternoons on television. It was easy to return his smile with that memory in mind. "Ma'am."

"Ally Jones, this is Deputy Warren Grover. I wanted to take a moment to introduce the two of you. In case, for whatever reason, you need to reach me and I'm not available, then Deputy Grover will be the one you'll most likely be talking to—and he'll do whatever he can to help you when I'm out of pocket. He's on a list of phone numbers that you'll find on the table at Primrose Inn."

"It's very nice to meet you, Deputy Grover. I hope I won't be a bother while I'm here."

"No bother at all, Miss Jones. We want to make sure you have a good stay while you're with us."

Matt put the vehicle into gear. "I'll be back for the council meeting, and we have the interview panel for the first county prosecutor applicants this afternoon, too. I'll be back after I see Miss Jones is settled in." They backed out of the space and the deputy gave a friendly wave of his hand in her direction.

"Everyone is so friendly. Is that the case with the entire town?" she couldn't help but ask.

"Well, I'd say it was pretty normal. People around here—and in general in small towns like ours, even though it is the county seat and busier than regular towns, people—will take a person at face value. Treat you with respect until you do something to lose that respect. They make good neighbors and good friends. Always eager to help out if they can. Don't feel like you're under a microscope or anything of that sort. They just find a newcomer in their midst and want to get to know you."

"Your town, what I've seen of it, is very pretty. I had it described to me over and over quite a few times by my friend. She may have made her home for many years in New York City, but her heart seemed to have been also very fond of this place." Ally stopped there. She hoped she had not opened the door for questions about Annie. The note she'd left Ally had more or less asked her to keep what she was doing for her to herself. As such, she wanted to honor her promise to the woman. "You and your sisters have lived here for a while as I understand it from Tori?"

"Tori came here first several years ago. She found a place to stay at the Primrose Inn, which was owned by a sweet lady who basically took her under her wing and welcomed her to Destiny's River. Tori decided it would make a good grounding point…a home…for all of us. We were in the foster care system for a while and then as each of us aged out, we decided how to make our paths. Tori kept the light on here, encouraging and praying that those paths would lead here. And so, they did, for myself and for my other sister, Cassie. You'll meet her soon enough. She and her husband are on a horse-buying trip, but they should be back next week. I'm sure Tori has told her all about you."

"And you have a brother who is not here."

"Right. He's still out there making his way in spite of the many words, calls, texts—you name it—of gentle and now more pointed encouragement from my two female siblings." He grinned at that, and Ally felt her breathing do a bit of a hiccup at the very pleasant sight. It softened his usual all-business countenance that she had come to expect, so when this side of him popped up, it made the moment memorable. She wasn't used to having anyone…especially a man…stir that amount of interest to be noticed by her brain, not for a long time.

Ally had never thought her looks were anything special. And the two or three men who had made it past the first coffee date to a second or third were nice and all, but nothing that had caused her heartbeat to accelerate. She often wondered if she had overlooked her chance while plowing the crowded streets of the city and missed that one special person Annie had said was out there…waiting for their paths to cross. Well, she had probably passed right by that person, if he did exist, and she would end up a spinster with a dog someplace she had yet to find. And she would be okay.

"And here we are…Primrose Inn. I hope you'll enjoy your time here."

The words brought her back to the present and she caught her breath as her gaze took in the large Victorian-style home that sat behind a white picket fence, its windows shining in the sunlight encompassed by shutters of bright yellow that stood out like sunshine itself against the stark white of the three-storied dwelling. There were two turrets with windows and two chimneys showing above the metal roof, which was a surprise to her. But the ornately carved wood pieces that framed the wide porch that ran the length of the front and could be seen in partial view toward the back through some shrubbery, made it appear something timeless and lovely and totally welcoming to one and all to stop and admire its beauty and its story.

"It is amazing. Like it should be in a fairy-tale book of its own," she breathed in total admiration. And then the reality that she would be staying in such a place for even a short period of time made it all the more incredible.

"You'll fit in perfectly with Tori and Cassie now," he said, exiting the vehicle and before she could grasp the handle, he was at her door and offering a hand to help her step out. "Those are words they say often, and each have set out to keep it as such. To fully appreciate it, you should see it when all the rose bushes are in full bloom in the garden, the bright wildflowers are in bloom in the flower beds and the shrubs have their own colors to add. Don't tell them I said so, but it is quite impressive and work is still in progress."

"I think it's perfect right now. I can't imagine what a beauty it must be in spring." She was so immersed in taking in everything about the yard, she wasn't aware that a helping hand had stayed at her elbow as they moved up the stone path to the wide front steps and made their way to the top. It remained there as he caught her gaze with his.

"You are really quite amazed by it. I'm guessing they have places like this where you come from, also?"

"Not like this. Houses and buildings of stone mostly. No room for yards and gardens like this…at least not in any neighborhood I've been in. Space is a premium in the city. This porch is so amazing."

"Well, if you like it now, just wait. It will be transformed this week into a fall country garden. Then, it's ablaze with lights and tinsel strung over anything and anyone who stands still too long. Again, be careful…my sisters will have you signed on to their nefarious crew of munchkins and elves before you know it. Shall we venture inside?"

Ally snapped back to reality. Her elbow was released easily enough. It had felt warm and secure, and she hadn't minded the touch. But he had other places to be and people to take care of. "I know you're too busy to stand around while I gawk like a silly girl. Please don't let me keep you from your work."

"Gawk away. I have some time." He held open the door after he punched in the code for the door. "All the information you need has been meticulously listed out for you in Volume One of Tori's notes which you can read at your leisure."

He held the door open, and she stepped through. Was that the smell of fresh-baked cookies? Oatmeal perhaps? She was immediately back in the apartment in New York, walking in from work and being greeted with fresh-baked goods that Annie had prepared for her. It made her heart squeeze, and she had to focus on the table in the dining room to her left.

But someone saw what she didn't want to be seen.

"Is there a problem? Something wrong?" His tone was low and quite genuine with his concern.

She shook her head. No use pretending otherwise. This lawman was able to see too much, too fast. She needed to remember that.

"Nothing wrong. Just a smell remembered from a past that is no more. A good memory just the same."

He looked as if he wanted to say more, but the moment passed. He crossed to the table and tapped the notebook with his finger. "This is Tori's long list of all the things you need to know and some you don't, but she is a politician after all… She gets carried away." He grinned that lovely grin again and she found how easy it was to respond with one of her own.

"I am sure it will all be helpful and it's so very thoughtful. I'll study it cover to cover."

"Follow me for the quick and yet expensive tour." He led and she did as she was told, admiring the beauty of wood and wainscoting and the furnishings that were heavy yet lighter-colored wood and with so many touches of colors here and there in pillows and rugs—and after the dining room and living room areas, came the kitchen at the back of the house and she stopped in the doorway. She felt she had stepped into one of those heavy coffee-table books on the art of country decorating. It was bright, large, filled with touches of copper and bright white granite cabinet tops and shipboard walls…and green ivy plants that were real and not fake. The windows were wide and looked out on the lawns and what appeared to be a gazebo and rose garden that was dormant at the moment. Double doors of glass panes opened onto another wide expanse of porch.

As if that wasn't enough, two barn doors opened onto what she could assume would be a sunroom…floor-to-ceiling windows went down both lengths and there was a highly polished floor and more tables and settees and inviting chairs with taller plants in the corners.

"I can't decide which room is more amazing—each one is better than the one before."

"This is a room that we added after Cassie's wedding. It serves as a nice large space for a reception or if the inn wants to add more visitors to any of the five bedrooms upstairs. This can become a dining room for meals to be served."

"Your sisters have thought of everything. It's all perfect. I don't quite understand why it isn't still used as an inn?"

"Tori never planned on having an inn to run when she

found Destiny's River. But that is what happened and that was what it was for a few years. Then she ran for office, met and married her husband. Then my other sister followed much the same road and added another husband to the family, and it just evolved into being a home place for all our growing family to gravitate to for special holidays and celebrations and such."

He smiled and his gaze stayed longer on hers. "And I think this has been quite an eventful morning for you and you need some of that rest that the doctor prescribed for you. You will find your suitcases and boxes are in the bedroom suite at the top of the stairs and to the right. You have both a view of the front yard and the back. Nice breeze in spring but not now. It's a bit too chilly in the evening now. You have all of our numbers. The code to the front door…and one more thing…" He rummaged in one of his pockets and drew out a key fob. He handed it over to her.

"There is a car in the garage for your use while you are here and for any of the errands you must run with Jillie and for shopping and whatever. It's yours to use however and whenever."

"That is so nice of you. And is Jillie's schedule in the book also?"

"It certainly is," he replied. "Along with maps marked of the various places you will become familiar with. And you won't have to begin with Jillie until Monday. Her schedule is there for each day. I am certain you will see Tori and Jillie at some point this weekend. But please don't be afraid to shoo them out and get that rest you need first and foremost. That is an order from the head law officer of this county. And people are wise to obey him."

"I see how you tried to keep a straight face there, but you might want to work on that little twitch at the corner of your mouth... It's a dead giveaway. People might not take you all that seriously with that going on."

The smile disappeared and she felt a bit sad to lose it.

"I can see I underestimated you. You need to be watched. A pretty, smart city girl is in our midst." He couldn't help it as that twitch appeared again. She had to smile.

"Thank you for everything you have done since I went airborne on your lovely county road. You and your family and so many others have done their best to help and welcome me. I'm not used to that, but it is very nice indeed."

He tapped his two fingers to the brim of his hat and allowed a grin to appear. "Get some rest and call if you need anything...and I mean anything at all." He walked down the hall, and she felt a bit of a letdown that he hadn't looked back just before stepping outside. But he probably had his mind already on his real job. And she was just a temporary employee that he had delivered instructions to and now she was on her own again. But she slowly retraced her steps and then went up to discover her room.

If she was a temporary employee, she would still feel like a princess thanks to the grand old house. She hugged Annie in her heart. She had a feeling she was smiling at that moment for her, too.

Chapter Nine

"ARE WE BORING you, Sheriff?"

The question was innocent enough, but given that it was from the mayor, his sister at that, it didn't exactly make him feel all that bad that he had been caught daydreaming out the window. He didn't look a bit contrite as he returned his attention to the four people around the meeting table. "Sorry all, but my mind was on another problem. And even then, I did hear your argument against the budget for the new drainage ditch along the east side of the football field, Mr. Walters. But given the amount of time my department alone has put in trying to redirect traffic around that part of the school and the adjacent neighborhood each time we get even a regular amount of rain, it will save money on that score alone. Plus, the fences along Mr. Jeffers' pasture go down with the onslaught of runoff and that allows his cattle to get to the stadium grounds, which again needs my office to become cowboys and round them up before anyone gets hurt or any damage is done to the field or to cars in the lots. It's a regular nuisance that has cost this county already several thousand dollars with no end in sight."

Tori smiled at her brother. *Nice save on that one.* But she secretly hoped his mind might be on other things…like Ally Jones. It wasn't a meeting that had kept him from picking

Ally up at the hospital and taking her to Primrose. She had a feeling her brother had figured that out by the way he shot her a look when he walked inside the door of her office for the meeting they were in at the moment. But she wasn't contrite either. She knew her brother better than most and there was something in the way he looked at and spoke to Ally Jones. She couldn't put her finger on it, but it was there. So it was up to her to help matters along if she could.

The discussion continued with the group agreeing to reconvene the following week and make final arguments and take a preliminary vote. "In a hurry, Sheriff? If you wouldn't mind staying for a minute or two?"

"A minute or two is about all I have, Mayor." He waited for the others to leave and then spoke up. "Yes, Ally Jones is settling into Primrose as we speak. She loved the house, and the cookies were a hit. She has the schedule and is studying it and will call with any questions. End of report. Now, I really do have work to do." He moved toward the door, but she was faster and stood in front of it.

"Thank you for handling that today…helping her get settled and all. She is really a sweet girl and Jillie seems to really like her, too. Maybe she'll like it so much here in Destiny's River that she'll want to stay even longer. Wouldn't that be nice?"

"You know why we never liked playing poker with you…my brother and sister and I?"

"Well, that was an unexpected response but I'm game. Why? I figured it was that you all were afraid I would beat you."

"We didn't want to beat you, big sister. You have a rotten poker face. We could tell in a heartbeat what you had in your hand and what you were up to—just like now."

"What do you mean? Now? I have a very good poker face. I'm a politician after all."

"Nice try. You, just like most other women around this town, are trying to push me or pull me or otherwise hog-tie me to one or another. Ally Jones will be gone after your maternity leave is done. And you need to help me to help Jillie remember that. I don't need my daughter's heart bruised when that happens. People come and go in life and this will just be another example. There is no future in thinking a big-city girl could ever be happy here in small-town Texas. Now, I do have work to do, and I would think so do you." He did stop long enough to plant a swift kiss on her forehead. She could infuriate him to no end sometimes, but she had raised him and their siblings when there wasn't anyone else. He would never forget that sacrifice.

☆

ALLY PUT AWAY her clothes in the huge closet, set out her toiletries in the large bathroom, and then helped herself to one of the homemade oatmeal cookies and a glass of the milk that had been supplied along with a wealth of other items according to the list…or Volume One as Matt had aptly named the list. It was certainly thorough and very helpful. Tori had highlighted each place that might be of more importance to Ally, including the vet's office and location for the GPS. That was the first thing Ally hoped to accomplish. She needed to see Teddy for herself and let him know she had not left him for good like his mistress had done them both.

After a shower and change of clothing, it felt good to put on some light makeup and run her own brush through her curls. She sat in front of the makeup mirror on the vanity in the dressing area of the walk-in closet and noted that the bruise was turning from a garish purple to an even more sickening brownish mustard. She worked to get some of the longer strands of hair to smooth over most of it. Not for the first time in her life did she look at her reflection. Her pluses were the sapphire-blue eyes and thick dark lashes—at least that's what people complimented her on. Some said they envied her the abundance of feathery golden-wheat blonde curls that was often unruly in her estimation, bouncing happily when she walked fast, and never seeming to change even when she ran her hand through them to try to tame them. She'd given up trying to subdue them and have a sleek hairstyle like so many other girls her age did. She had a nose referred to as 'pert' and a complexion Annie called peaches and cream. Probably trying in her sweet way to always be uplifting and kind. At least she had a petite figure with suitably comment-worthy curves in the right places.

"It is what it is," she told her image in the mirror. She chose a pair of slim-fitting brown slacks and a long-sleeved sweater with a cowl neck in a mixture of browns and greens. The tiny gold studs were in her ears where they had been since the birthday two years ago when Annie had presented them to her. The tiny gold cross with a wreath of gold flowers around it hung on a fine chain at her neck. It was with her always also. She had been called sentimental a time or two in her life and she had no problem with that. She didn't have much of anything to claim as her own, but what she did have was very meaningful to her. And more cherished to her than others felt about their jewels and fancy clothes or trips or ornate houses. It was the people, notably Annie, who were worth all of that to her and more.

She found her purse in one of the boxes gathered up from the wreck site. And she had quickly checked to make certain that the carved box was still sealed and intact that she was entrusted in delivering to Destiny's River. That brought a sigh of relief when she found it in another box. Gathering her notebook and key fob, she went into the garage and found a small red SUV that looked to be almost brand new. In fact, it barely had two thousand miles on it. And it drove like a dream. She was going to be spoilt when she got her old car back...if she did. That was a conversation and visit for tomorrow with the mechanic.

Traffic was nothing compared to the city she came from. And there was a wonderful absence of blaring horns and people yelling at each other and getting nowhere in the gridlock. It took her all of fifteen minutes to locate the vet's office on a side street down a block or two from the courthouse and center of the town. Pulling her bag over her shoulder, she pushed through the door of the building and immediately was welcomed by the light barks and meows of a veterinary office. They were only overshadowed by the smiling welcome and greetings from the two vet techs at the front desk. She told them who she was and explained that she was there to see her dog.

"Oh, you're Teddy's person," one of the girls piped up

with a huge grin. "He is such a little love. I'll take you back to see him."

The cleanliness of the place was a surprise. And she was surprised by the number of people working in the back, moving quickly here and there and animals that were also moving…some in cages, some in arms, but everywhere there seemed to be people and animals on a mission. A tall man in blue scrubs came out of one of the doors and he nodded. "Hello, I'm Dr. Adams. I bet you're Ally Jones?" He shook her hand.

"Well, yes, I am."

"You are just as Matt described you. He told me we would probably be seeing you if not today, first thing in the morning."

"I wanted to check on Teddy and let him know I didn't abandon him."

"Well, he has had a very thoughtful visitor each day like clockwork. And I am expecting to see her come through that door in the next ten minutes. So why don't we get you situated in one of our free rooms and bring Teddy in for a reunion?"

He nodded at the tech who had escorted her from the front. The girl took off down a side hallway. The doctor indicated she should follow him. The room was nice and spacious with a full-length window that looked out on a wide expanse of fenced yard where there were trees for shade and benches for sitting. A couple of larger dogs were visible outside with one of the techs enjoying some exercise. "I was feeling bad for Teddy being locked up, so to speak, but this is a very nice place. And I thank you for all you did for him.

I don't know what I would have done if he had been seriously hurt or worse. He and I are what's left of our family."

The man nodded. "I totally understand that. But once we get that pin removed from his ankle area, he should be good as new. Maybe a little limp in colder weather…but then I do that with my old bones too," he said and laughed. She did the same. The door opened about that time and the tech came in carrying the furry animal. When he caught sight of Ally, he couldn't wait to get from the arms that held him to Ally's.

"Settle down, my sweetheart. I'm here now. Everything is good," she crooned in a soft voice to the bouncing ball of fur. She was trying to be mindful of the pin that she had been told was visible and it was anchored in the bones. She looked up at the vet.

"It is sturdier than it looks but we do try to keep him calmer than this. However, this is a special occasion. He will calm down in a couple of minutes. Just let him lie on the table and you can talk to him. If all progresses as it should, I think he can go with you tomorrow afternoon, if he is kept reasonably quiet, no jumping off things or chasing rabbits or rough play. Couch time is good. Being even more spoilt than I think he already is. We'll have instructions for you, and we have an on-call rotation twenty-four/seven so we can help whenever needed."

There was a light tap on the door, and then Jillie stuck her head around it. Her face lit up when she saw both Teddy and Ally together. She joined them beside the table. Teddy had to smother her in licks a few times.

"He's so happy you're here now," Jillie said to Ally. "I

told him you were coming soon."

"And I'm so glad you kept him company and kept him from being sad. You helped him heal by doing that…you helped both of us."

"Well, isn't this a great sight? You two are united once more." Tori had slipped into the room after Jillie. She joined them and added a pat for Teddy, also.

"He is the center of attention and eating it up," the vet said. "But I think we can let him settle down a bit before his dinner does get served. He will need to rest up for his trip out of here tomorrow."

"He's going tomorrow?" Jillie seemed a bit sad but happy for him, too.

Ally smiled. "Yes and remember you'll see a lot of him still when you're at Primrose in the afternoons. You guys will still be best buddies."

"That's true! I'm so glad you and Teddy came to Destiny's River. And I hope you two will stay forever."

"That makes three of us," Tori spoke up. "Now let's go, Miss Jillie. You have homework to get done so you won't have to waste your weekend time with it. Your dad will drop you at Tiffany's. And don't let us forget your bag is in my car and he needs to take it and you to Tiffany's."

"I'm going to a sleepover tonight. But I'll be home after lunch tomorrow. In case you need help bringing Teddy home or anything."

"I'll keep that in mind. It sounds like you'll be having a fun evening. Good for you." Ally was touched when Jillie gave Teddy a hug and then she turned and wrapped her arms around Ally's waist, giving her a quick hug too. Then she was gone. Tori gave her a quick wink and told her and Doc bye before she left at a slower pace for an expectant mom.

"You met some good people there in the Lockwoods and Parkers. The ones you haven't yet met are just as fine, too. Now, don't you worry. Teddy will be ready tomorrow afternoon."

"I can't thank you enough, Dr. Adams, I hope you know how much this little dog means to me. I couldn't lose him now."

"I have a pretty good idea of what you two mean to each other. And you might as well call me Doc—everyone in town does."

Ally gave Teddy a goodbye hug and he seemed to have found his lopsided grin again. He shared it with her as he was carried away by the vet tech. Ally stopped at the front desk before leaving.

"Yes, ma'am, Miss Jones." She was greeted with the same friendliness as earlier. "How can we help?"

"If you would tell me what the bill amount is for Teddy? I get to take him home tomorrow and I just want to check on it now?"

The receptionist pulled up the screen on her computer and studied it. "Well, it seems the bill has been taken care of already."

Ally shook her head. "You must have me confused with someone else in your accounts. I haven't paid yet."

The young lady shook her head. "No, it's a zero balance. It looks to have been billed and paid yesterday."

"By whom?"

"I'm sorry but I don't have permission to give out that

information. The person chose to not have it released. I'm sorry. But it must be nice to have such a surprise."

Ally could only nod and smile a thank you to the receptionist. And as soon as her brain got over the shock of the news, it came up with a likely Good Samaritan. She would find out and pay that person back. Her next stop was D and J Garage.

As soon as she pulled up and parked, she saw a familiar sight. Her little car was hoisted up on a lift inside one of the bays. Surely, they weren't working on it. They might still be checking it out for an estimate. That is what she asked for when she was able to give them a call after her phone had been delivered to the hospital after the accident.

She walked inside the office part of the building, and a woman came out of another smaller office to greet her.

"How may we help you?"

"I'm Ally Jones and…" She got no further.

"Yes, ma'am…nice to meet you." The woman smiled and held out her hand and they shook. "I'm Dee…the D in D and J," she said with a laugh. "I'm the one who did the estimate, and we just got the parts in we needed so your little car is being started today. I had to tell you because of its age, we had to send a distance for one or two things we needed. But we got them."

"It's nice to meet you. You've already started? I never received an estimate."

"Well, we were given a green light, and the bill has been taken care of already. So, you don't have to worry on that score. And we will guarantee our work. No need to worry about that, either."

"Let me guess," Ally responded, already having an idea of the answer, "the person who paid wants to remain anonymous?"

Dee winked at her. "Yes, indeed. You are one lucky lady. Although, I'm not surprised. I heard you were a very pretty lady from up north."

Ally had to admire the woman's forthright speech and attitude. "Up north?"

"I don't mean to be politically incorrect or nothing, but up north generally refers to those people from the East Coast… Yankees for want of a better term."

Ally could not help herself. She had to laugh. She shook her head trying to tame it down to a grin. "I'm not laughing at you. I just haven't heard that term in ages. Someone I knew once, a dear friend, said that and I laughed then also. I take no offense. I am learning that Texas is a lot like its own country."

"Well, we were indeed our own country a couple hundred years or so ago. But just so you know we aren't being snobs or such."

"I don't take it that way. Let's just pretend that I came in here with a car in pretty much the same shape as my car is in…what would be a ballpark figure do you think?"

"Smart lady. Brains and pretty. And if I came across a car in that shape…well, let's see." Dee scribbled on a piece of paper and turned it around for her to see. Ally took a silent but deep breath in. "I see. Thanks for that ballpark idea."

"No problem," the woman said and tossed the paper into the trash. "We'll give you a call when it can be picked up, but it might take a week or more. Just depends on if there is something else we can't see yet."

"I will leave it in your mechanic's expert hands."

"Well, I do like having my hands called expert."

Ally smiled. "You're my mechanic?"

Dee beamed back at her. "Yes, indeed. My daughter Jaimie and I are the D and J in the sign. My dad taught us both and his dad taught him and so forth."

"I do love that fact. I know my car is in excellent hands. Thank you."

"You have a good day and welcome to Destiny's River. Hope you do stay a while."

Ally nodded and smiled her thanks.

She pulled the car out of the parking lot. And she knew of one direction she needed to head…to the heart of the town.

Chapter Ten

"HOW MAY WE help you?"

The deputy was female and greeted Ally as she approached the long counter that separated the large area. She had found a parking space across the street from the courthouse, which seemed to be a busy place on a Friday afternoon. She hoped it would be easy to find the sheriff's office and it was. She entered through the heavy wooden door with its frosted glass with the wording across its pane and Matthew Parker denoted as the sheriff underneath the larger letters. Stepping inside, she saw a half dozen people, all in uniform and in various stages of work. The female deputy was obviously in charge of the incoming visitors.

"I don't have an appointment, and don't know if I needed one or not, but I had hoped to have a few minutes...not even five if that...of the sheriff's time?"

"The sheriff is very busy, and an appointment is..." the woman replied but was interrupted by a taller, male deputy whom Ally recognized. He had approached with a smile on his face.

"An appointment is not necessary for Miss Jones, Deputy Lozano."

"You're Miss Jones," the woman responded and her officious face became more friendly with a smile creasing it. "I'm sorry."

"I'll take over," Deputy Grover said to his counterpart.

"Nice to meet you, ma'am," the deputy said as she departed. "Welcome to Destiny's River."

"Thank you," Ally responded, a bit confused as to how people knew of her before she even met them.

"I'm sorry to be just dropping in like this but I didn't know the protocol and since I was in town and down the block, I thought I might see if I could have a word with Sheriff Parker. But I understand if he is too busy."

"Is it something I could help you with?"

"I really need to talk to him about it. It is more of a personal thing about the accident." She didn't know how else to use to describe it.

"I understand. I'm sure he wouldn't mind the interruption at all. He is just across the street but let me check in with him. Just a moment." He stepped away a short distance and touched a button on the small mike attached to his shoulder. He responded to the reply and moved back to the counter.

"I'll escort you to where the sheriff is. He's just finishing up a meeting with some of our citizens." He grabbed his hat off the hat rack beside the doorway and then held the door open for her. She was surprised to find they were exiting the courthouse and heading to the crosswalk that would get them to the opposite side of the street from the building.

"I was under the impression his meeting was in the courthouse," she ventured when they made it to the sidewalk and traffic could continue its way behind them.

"It is a late lunch meeting that then moved into another

meeting for coffee, and that meeting just ended, so he's probably looking forward to a bit of a change right about now," the deputy explained. They came to the door of Tillie's, and he held it open for her to enter. Even late in the afternoon, she was surprised there would be quite a few tables still taken in the café. It was pleasant and the décor was pure gingham, red and blue, with white carnations surprisingly fresh on the center of the tables. And it smelled of baked goods and juicy hamburgers, which reminded her that she had not stopped for lunch but had only had two oatmeal cookies before leaving Primrose. The deputy nodded and spoke to several people as he led the way to a booth, around the corner and with a restricted view of the rest of the room. Matt Parker stood at their approach. She was struck again by the man's good looks. Something she had really never paid much heed to in the city. Maybe it was something about the country air?

"Thanks, Deputy," he said and nodded to the man. "Why don't you take a plate of those muffins Tillie just took out of the oven back to the office? The crew deserves something on a Friday afternoon. It's already on my account."

"I'll do that and thanks. Nice to meet you again, Miss Jones." He nodded to her and then left them.

Matt indicated the other side of the booth with his hand. "Please have a seat. I hope you don't mind coming over here. Much quieter and gives me a small breather before the next item on my list."

Ally slid into the booth and folded her hands together on the tabletop in front of her. She was about to speak, but a waitress appeared with another glass of water for the sheriff and a small plate with four muffins on it. She sat another small plate with a fork in front of each of them. She smiled at Ally. "What can I get you to drink? Coffee goes well with these fresh banana nut muffins."

"You have to try Tillie's muffins," Matt spoke up. "They are their own food group they're so good."

She didn't want to seem ill-mannered, so she nodded and requested coffee. The woman disappeared.

"I'm sorry about just dropping by without an appointment. It certainly won't take long to say what I need to say. And I hate interrupting you while you have time for a quick break. Deputy Grover said you've had quite a busy day so far."

The coffee arrived and then they were alone, except for customers at the two tables across the room, who Ally hadn't paid attention to when she arrived.

"It's fairly typical, but we do have our Fall Fest coming up rather soon and the committees need some supervision or a neutral party…depending on who is on what committee." He grinned along with the comment.

"It sounds like much the same thing as our committees back in the city. Our church ladies could be quite stubborn and territorial."

"Then you know why I seek quiet refuge away from my office." He offered the plate of muffins to her. "Please try a couple of these—they're still warm. How about some butter with them?"

"Just one." She slid it on her plate. "No butter." He was clearly waiting for her pronouncement on the delicacy. She took a fork and slid a bit into her mouth. And then she decided a second fork might be worthwhile. He smiled at her.

"I thought so. You only thought a bite would do it. Take the second one." And he moved it onto her plate. "Because if you don't take it, then I would have to eat three so that Tillie's feelings wouldn't be hurt."

"And I can see how worried you are about that happening," she said, eyeing him with a bit of sarcasm. She took another bite.

"I'll share a secret with you. But you must keep it to yourself. Don't want it getting out."

"I'm intrigued," she whispered back in the same tone he had used.

"On Wednesday and Friday afternoons, about this time, stop in here and you'll find some warm muffins, different flavors depending on her mood that day, but you can grab a couple of nice warm muffins and a beverage and make it through the rest of your afternoon."

"I shall certainly remember that. Thank you for sharing. Now how about sharing something else with me?"

Matt placed his fork down and gave her his attention. "Sounds important. I take it that's why you stopped to see me?"

"It is." She sat up straighter in the booth, her plate empty, and gaze met gaze. "I went to the vet's office and had a great visit with Teddy and Doc. He did ask that I call him that. Very nice man. His whole staff, or the ones I met at any rate, seemed very caring also. Then I stopped at D and J and met Dee who is quite a friendly and nice character in her own right."

"I'm glad that you found them all to be welcoming. We do have good people here."

"Yes, and they told me the same thing in both places. When I asked the amount of the bill that I owed, they said nothing. They told me that someone...and neither of them would say who...but someone had paid both bills already."

"Really?"

"Makes one speechless, doesn't it?" She continued to watch him.

"I suppose it does. Why did you need to speak to me about that?"

"I was hoping you could use some of your police detecting experience and find out the guilty party for me? I certainly want to thank them personally."

"Well...maybe they didn't want these people to share that information because they don't want anything in return?"

"Why? I know it was you. I'm a stranger here...a stranger to all of the people here. Why would you or anyone take care of those bills?"

"It's the right thing to do. As I see it...it's my daughter's fault that all the things were set in motion with her running into that road. And you could only react. Your car was damaged. Your dog was hurt. And you spent three days in the hospital. My daughter learned a hard lesson about actions and consequences. But she's alive because of your split-second decision. So, if I choose to pick up a few bills, it's nothing compared to what you did. And all you need to do is say thanks and let it go."

"That's all?"

"Can I get you two anything else? Freshen up your cups?"

"I think we're good," Matt said to the woman who walked up to the table, with a carafe of fresh coffee in her hand. "Tillie, may I introduce Ally Jones from—"

"New York City," she finished the sentence for him with a big smile at Ally. "News travels faster than a proverbial speeding bullet in a small town. We're glad to have you visiting us."

"Thank you. And those muffins were excellent."

"I appreciate that. I'm not sure if or how often those and other pastries will be coming out of the kitchen. Marvin, the genius behind those goodies is leaving for a couple of months. He's heading back to California to help his mother sell their business now that his father has died, and his mom needs to go live with her daughter. So, I'll be looking for someone to come in on a limited basis in case either of you come across anyone who can turn out great baked goods three days a week."

"I'll pass the word," Matt responded. "Hope you find someone soon."

"Well, I better get back to work. I hear the boss is a real slave driver around here," she said with a laugh that Matt joined in with.

"If you'll excuse me for a second?" Ally stood and headed in the direction of the ladies' room. Once out of sight from their table, she stepped to the counter for a few words with Tillie. Then, that business concluded, she made her way back to where Matt waited. She remained standing, and so he stood also.

"Thanks for the muffins and for everything else. But I'll find a way to pay you back."

"Are you settling in at Primrose? Anything else you need there?"

"Nothing yet. But I'll let you know if there is. And I'll be ready for Monday when I take over for your sister."

"I'll walk out with you." Ally couldn't help notice that there were more than a few tables scattered through the café with patrons whose glances in her direction were more than a little interested. She never liked being the center of attention, but she guessed she would have to get used to it. Matt held the door for her, and she was glad to step outside.

"It's like being in a fishbowl. But people will move on to something else." Matt had noticed, too. Ally was glad about that. It verified it wasn't just her imagination.

"Your sister told me a little about your particular situation."

That stopped the man, and he turned to look at her with a question in his eyes. He voiced it. "My sister Tori has been discussing me. What situation would that be?"

"I believe she said you're having more than your fair share of attention from the single ladies of this town?"

"You are definitely a person who speaks what's on her mind. Guess that's what city girls do?"

"Don't know about all city girls, so I can't speak to that. But my voice works just fine."

Matt couldn't help but smile. "That's good to know. Now, I just have to get my sisters to stay out of my business and stop sharing it with others."

"Judging by the looks we're getting standing out here

talking together—" she ventured a brief look around the sidewalk and traffic easing along between stop lights "—people are watching but trying to be inconspicuous about it. Which only makes it more obvious. It's a look that was probably refined in the subways of New York and found its way even to Texas." She said all of that while keeping a broad smile on her face. She gave a tilt of the head as she looked up at him.

"She also said that I could help out and give you a buffer for a while. And I didn't give credence to that until today. You paid my bills, and I do owe you for what you are doing right now to help me out. Consider it quid pro quo or simply paying back by helping."

"You think smiling like that at me on a town sidewalk will help the cause?"

She nodded. "It can't hurt. But I warn you I'm not all that experienced in the art of flirting. So, I might just get it all wrong."

Matt shook his head. "I can't quite believe that about you not being experienced. You're making a good start at it. But it's not necessary to go along with any silly idea that my sister cooked up just as a means of payback."

"Save your breath, Sheriff. I pay my debts, and this is a big one. I can go along with it while I'm here. Then you'll have to think of another way to sidestep your admirers."

"You're probably wondering what you've gotten yourself into coming to this little town in Texas. You'll be in a hurry to see the last of us."

Ally looked around at the sidewalks with people passing each other and smiling in greeting…even at her—a total stranger earlier that day. The vehicles with drivers raising a friendly hand in passing one another...no blaring horns, no people too busy to notice each other. Would she be glad to see the last of them? A strange feeling passed through her at the thought. Annie had told her about Destiny's River and the people and the way you could feel the pull of belonging and home. She had dismissed much of it as an older woman's exaggerated memory recall. But now she was beginning to re-examine some of those notions.

Matt walked her to her vehicle and soon she was on her way back to Primrose Inn. What had possessed her to speak up in such a way? To state she was willing to go along with Tori's idea. All she knew was that she was possibly grasping at straws after realizing it would be difficult to pay back the debt to Matt Parker even if he said he didn't want it. She had learned hard work and to pay for what she had...never to be in debt to someone or something else if she could help it.

It was times like these that she sorely wished Annie was still around to share her wisdom with her. She wasn't ready to have lost her. The woman had been her anchor, her best friend, and the only family she had...even though they weren't blood. But Annie had said that the luckiest families were those who could choose their members. Ally agreed.

Chapter Eleven

"RIGHT ON TIME." Doc Adams smiled at Ally as she stepped into the exam room the next afternoon. "And if I didn't know better, Teddy knows what time it is, too. He has been sitting by the door of the play area watching each person who walks by. I would say he is more than ready to get out and about."

"I'm more than ready for him to come back to me, also. I have his bed ready, bowls, the food you prescribed, and the front desk already gave me his meds and the daily instructions."

"Good job." The door opened and Teddy couldn't be contained in the tech's arms he was squirming so much once he spotted Ally.

The tech handed him over and Ally gave him a fierce hug and laughed as he rained dog kisses along her cheek. The vet held the door and walked her and Teddy out to the waiting room.

All the way to their temporary digs, Ally talked, filling in the dog sitting in the passenger seat, secured in his pet harness, who seemed to be attentive to every word. He also was intent on checking out the passing scenery. "You have a yard, fenced, with grass and plenty of room to explore. No more dog parks and big dogs giving you a hard time. It will be quite a vacation for you, too."

She pulled the car into the drive and parked. "Here we are," she announced. "It's like a mansion, isn't it? Just don't go getting too used to such things. We won't be able to afford anything quite so nice when we leave here. But let's get you in and settled—almost time for your meds."

It was clear that Teddy agreed with their surroundings. After a brief tour, he settled down on the comfy cushioned bed she had just bought. It was close to a window so that he could get some afternoon sun to induce sleep. Ally changed into jeans and a bright blue pullover sweater, comfy sneakers and then decided to make up a batch of peanut butter cookies. They would be good for after-school snacks when her part-time job began the next day. Jillie liked them according to page three of Tori's instructions. That made Ally smile even more. The first batch went into the oven and she was checking for ingredients for some homemade stew when the doorbell sounded.

To her surprise, Jillie stood there, and her dad was right behind her. "Sorry we dropped by without calling first. But I picked up Jillie from choir and she kept on and on about checking on Teddy and all. I made a deal with her that we would stop for five minutes if she would eat all her vegetables at dinner."

"I see." Ally grinned at the girl who made a grimace at her dad's words. "The bribery angle. I've been there myself a few times at your age. Come on in. Teddy is in the living room."

Jillie didn't need to be told twice. She was off in a flash. Matt stepped into the entryway and took the hall more slowly. "Thanks for being a sport about this."

"Jillie can come visit anytime. Although, with her being here during the week or whatever, she might grow tired of it."

Jillie and Teddy were busy with a ball that had been a new purchase for Teddy's homecoming. Ally and Matt watched for a few moments.

"Is something burning?" Matt looked in the direction of the kitchen.

"Oh no! My cookies." Ally moved quickly down the hall, with Matt following a few steps behind. Grabbing her oven mitts, she opened the oven door and reached inside. She was in a rush and the edge of the mitt allowed a strip of skin to come into contact with the side of the oven. That caused her to drop the cookie sheet onto the open door and send cookies sliding onto the floor. Luckily, half of them stayed on the pan on the oven door. In a split second, Matt had grabbed her elbow and moved her to stand in front of the sink, cold water rushing over the site.

"Burn ointment?"

Ally got her mind back in focus and nodded under the sink. "I saw some under the sink earlier and a small first aid kit. It's okay, it was just a shock, and I can handle it."

But he was already gently tamping off the water from the site with a paper towel. Then he opened the tube of ointment and spread some on the burn. He blew on the area gently to lessen any sting. It made Ally jerk her arm at the unexpected sensation on her lower arm. It was surprising and strangely pleasant. He looked up at her, still holding her arm. Ally wanted to say something, but nothing came to mind, which made her feel silly.

"We can put light gauze over it or let it breathe for a while. It's painful but that will fade soon enough."

"I feel so clumsy. And the cookies…just a few left that are edible. I know they're Jillie's favorite…thanks to your sister…and wanted to have them for tomorrow for my first time taking over her after-school care."

"That's thoughtful of you. But don't beat yourself up over it. You have a few and that will be fine for Monday and probably the next day, too. Nothing has changed about your plans."

"Is this why people think you make a good sheriff? You stay calm when others do not. You know first aid, and you know how to deal with a woman who suddenly makes little sense on how far a half dozen cookies will go. Nice defusing of a potentially hysterical cook."

The grin he gave her, so up close and perfect, allowed her to note the deep grooves on either side of a strong male mouth above a squared chin that was drawing her attention and doing things with her brain waves. She was seeing why he was high on so many women's lists.

"All in a day's work," he responded. "Tori called and said she had talked to you about meeting you at the school and just making sure you met teachers and such. She'll come there right after her checkup, but she should be on time."

Ally's elbow was hers again and she picked up a spatula and began plating the surviving cookies. It gave her something to focus on besides the man leaning against the cabinet watching her. "No problem. She's really being so helpful. I hope she won't worry about Jillie and me too much. In spite of burning myself and ruining most of the cookies, I really am trustworthy."

"If either one of us felt you were anything less, you wouldn't have been our choice, no matter the alternatives. But your references spoke very highly of you and you have experience with kids. So a few ruined cookies won't be a deal breaker. Now, I need to get my daughter home and ready for another week at school." He pushed away from the counter and headed back down the hall and she followed.

"Okay, Jilliebean, let's get moving. I'm sure you'll see a lot of Teddy."

"Bye, Teddy," she said giving her furry friend a last hug. "I can't wait for Monday, Miss Ally. It's going to be awesome having you come to my school."

"Bye, Jillie," she replied, following them both onto the porch. "Be careful and see you tomorrow!" She returned Jillie's wave as the truck backed from the driveway.

She didn't return to the house right away. Dusk was falling and streetlights were beginning to glow. Leaves were being picked up from along the street and chasing each other over pavement and sidewalks. There was a definite drop in temperature, and she folded her arms against the chill. The smell of woodsmoke from chimneys brought thoughts of her life back east. And thoughts of Annie and their time together. A sense of loneliness in the strange new place where she'd traveled to fulfill a woman's last wish mingled in the quiet night. A remembered warmth on an elbow stayed in the recesses of her mind, chasing the gloom away. Tomorrow would come without fail.

Just as she had done each evening since Annie left her,

first in New York and then in Destiny's River, she paused beside the table near the front window in the parlor of the inn. The carved box sat there where Ally would gently run her hand over the wood and close her eyes and send a simple prayer and good night to the woman she had promised to return to Destiny's River. Her promise would soon be complete.

☆

"THERE SHE IS! There's Miss Ally." Jillie's hand went up in a wave. "Here we are!"

"I was afraid I'd be late," Ally said, as she reached the trio watching her approach.

"You're right on time," Matt responded. "Ally Jones, this is Mrs. King, Allie's homeroom teacher."

"Hello, Mrs. King, it's nice to meet Jillie's teacher." The two women shook hands.

Matt caught the look of surprise at his presence as she had walked toward them. "I know Tori was supposed to be here with you, but she's in the hospital. Her doctor did the routine checkup, but he sent her right over to the hospital. Her BP was elevated, and he wanted to be on the safe side so close to her due date. So I'm her stand-in."

"I totally understand. I hope she and the baby will be okay," Abby told him.

"They're in good hands." He then looked at his daughter who had moved to stand beside Ally, a proud grin on her face. "How about you show her where your classroom is and then where you'll be when she picks you up?"

"That is a good idea." Mrs. King smiled. "And we can visit a few minutes afterwards."

Ally nodded. "Sounds good." She turned to Matt. "It's okay. I know you're busy. I think Jillie and I will be just fine. Don't stay on my account."

Stay on my account. As he drove away from the school and headed back to his office, the words kept repeating in his head. He was trying to be helpful. Tori had suggested it in the first place, and he wanted to help out his sister. That was why he had taken time to be there. And for Jillie…this was something new in her routine. But he knew that Jillie had barely noticed his presence once Ally had arrived. Stay on her account? Ally Jones's account? Of course, he was helping. That's what he did. *Sure, it is.*

And now he was mocking himself. He was too smart to be buying into Tori's half-baked idea about throwing a smoke screen up using the presence of Ally Jones helping them out for the time she was with them. It was thin at best. It didn't take the woman too long to see right through it herself. But she had agreed. Agreed because she felt she owed a debt and wanted to pay it back. She was smart and tough and caring and good with Jillie and beautiful…inside and outside. Anyone but a blind man could figure that one out. She came from a huge city, traveling alone with only a dog as a companion. Because a dear friend had asked her to do so. She had commitment and kept to her word. And that was a rare commodity. All of that only served to keep her as an enigma in his mind. One that was strangely taking root.

Four days into the week, Matt felt a routine had materialized automatically. Each afternoon, Jillie was picked up at the designated time by Ally. Then, depending on the day and activity, they had made it to choir practice at the church, piano lessons, and dance lessons. Homework had been finished by the time he picked up his daughter. Jillie ran out the door, usually when he pulled in the driveway and Ally waved at them from the porch. Not many chances to catch up on anything. But the weekend was approaching.

In fact, he had decided to take the initiative and invite Ally to join him and Jillie for dinner at the café. But his sister had other plans in mind. Her call alerted him to such before he could call Ally with his idea.

"Hey, little brother of mine," she began with her usual greeting and then launched right into the purpose of her call: "I've made plans for Jillie and Ally to meet us at the café for one last supper, so to speak, before the doctor throws me into the hospital and gives this stubborn kid inside me no more time to procrastinate. It would be convenient for you to walk over and join us. Isn't that a great idea? We plan on six thirty p.m. sharp in order to beat the dinner crowd. I've got to run but we'll see you then." And that was that.

Matt shook his head. Leave it to his sister to still be ramrodding plans for them. He should be tired of it, but instead, he had to smile. Tori was one of a kind. He loved her dearly and didn't know what he would have done without her in their lives when they lost their parents as children. And she had raised them, albeit in foster care, and they were able to stick together. And then when Jillie came along, and he lost his wife…well that had been really tough, but she'd stepped in…as did his other two siblings…and they kept moving forward one day at a time. So, he would cut her some slack.

Besides, it worked well that he would get a little more time with Ally Jones…to catch up on the week with Jillie. That was the reason he told himself. And it was a good one.

He walked across the street about ten minutes before the appointed time. He was going to be early and get a table for their group. He should have known better. Matt stepped into the café and was met with the sight of his sister already waving at him from a table toward the far side of the room. And she wasn't alone. Jillie stood up and ran to his side, giving him a quick hug.

"Hi, Dad." She beamed up at him. "We beat you here. Isn't this fun?"

He returned the hug and grinned. "Yes, you beat me. And yes, this is a fun idea." They made their way over to where his sister and her husband were already seated, along with Ally. Jillie slid into a chair next to Ally but there was an empty one on the other side of her, and he sat down there. It wasn't lost on him given the knowing smile on her face that Tori had planned the seating arrangements and was pleased with the outcome. He chose to ignore her, shaking hands across the table with his brother-in-law, Caden Lockwood.

"This is a special occasion having all of you here together. Is it a special celebration or something?" Tillie asked, giving an even brighter smile and a wink in his direction. Matt turned his attention to the menu. Caden took on the conversation.

"It's just a nice dinner out. A dinner with family before Tori's anchored to the house for a few weeks with our little guy."

"How nice! And it's a growing family. Indeed," Tillie

replied. Her smile brightened as it landed on Ally and then ended with Matt.

The woman busied herself for the next few minutes taking their orders and serving their drinks and salads. Once she had left, Matt caught his sister's gaze and leaned closer to where she sat next to him at the table to whisper his comment. "I'm surprised you haven't rented a billboard at the town's city limits and placed the news on the town's radio marketplace."

Tori glanced at the other occupants at the table. Caden had engaged Jillie and Ally in regaling their agenda of the day and so she whispered back: "I find that unnecessary as things are progressing just fine on the gossip hotline. And after this evening, it will be buzzing with even greater activity. Cade's words just now about our lovely family dinner were a stroke of genius, even if I didn't encourage him. We've got you covered, and you should have a peaceful few weeks. You feel free to thank me as much as you like."

"Thanks, is not what I would call the words in my brain for you right now." Matt turned his attention back to the others. Ally was smiling at something Jillie said, and Cade seemed intent on watching the pair also. Or was it Ally where his attention was caught and held? Strange. It had to be that he was imagining it. Matt knew that his sister and her husband met in what people described as a fairy-tale way and were more in love and happy than ever. Couldn't be that a green-eyed monster was playing with his thoughts. *Ridiculous.* There was nothing to be jealous about. Tori's crazy ideas and plan were rubbing off on him. He would maintain his grasp on sanity.

The food began to arrive, and conversation was general. Dinner progressed in a leisurely manner. Matt watched as Jillie and Ally seemed to have a natural friendship growing. Ally Jones had come along and somehow it felt she had always been there, fitting so seamlessly into the fabric of their lives and the town. And he felt a danger sign. What happened when she left? She had made it plain that she was only stopping long enough to visit the place her dear friend had talked of so often. Then what? She would just leave? And what about Jillie? What if she became too close to the woman? Would it be another heartbreak? He had done his best to protect his little girl from that since she lost her mother. And that had included himself.

"Why the frown all of a sudden? Something wrong with your dinner?" Tori was looking at him with concern. The last thing he needed was to have his know-all, see-all, fix-all big sister suspicious.

"Just thinking about a case that I have some work to do on this weekend. Just tying up loose ends." He could play it off as work.

"If you need me out of your hair, I could always go over to Ally's and help her bake," Jillie piped up.

"Yes." Ally nodded. "I do have a couple new recipes to work on. Extra hands are always good."

Matt shook his head. "You have my daughter all week. You do get to have some time off."

"I do mean it." Ally spoke up. "She's a good helper and it's just me and Teddy in that big, beautiful house. So, the offer is always open."

"And I think this is where I should apologize," Tori said.

"I'm afraid some of that work in the kitchen might be my fault. Having this baby right before the Fall Fest and all, I just added more responsibilities to your list."

Ally shook her head. "Don't worry about that. I think it's fun. I'm glad to help Ally and her school out."

Matt was lost. "Ally and her school? What's this about the Fall Fest?"

"Ally has stepped into my empty shoes with helping for the Fall Fest. She's in charge of the baked goods for Ally's class."

"I had no idea. You didn't need to agree to do that," Matt said, feeling he should have been more aware of what was going on with Jillie's school and the class participation. Tori always stepped in, but he had no idea that it was falling to Ally now.

"I can buy items from the café here and the bakery, too. You certainly don't need to spend your time, let alone funds, to take on extra projects."

Tori grinned. "Well, I think we need dessert right now, speaking of baked goods. I took the liberty of ordering a slice of chocolate pie for you, Matt. We all know that's your favorite."

"Since when is there chocolate pie here at Tillie's?"

"Since she discovered this amazing new baker. The same one who does those cinnamon rolls you've been raving about with your morning coffee meetings at the courthouse this past week."

"And he does indeed rave about those," Tillie added, with a tray of desserts in hand. She placed strawberry cream pies in front of Tori and Jillie, coconut cream in front of Ally and Cade. And an amazing chocolate slice in front of Matt.

"What do you think?" Tori prompted him, with the others smiling in wait for his pronouncement.

"Well, it looks almost too good to eat." The topping of cream was a good inch thick and then curlicues of chocolate adorned the top. It looked appetizing. The first forkful went into his mouth. And then another one.

"Don't keep us in suspense, man," Cade prompted, a bite of his cream pie waiting on his fork.

"This is amazing," Matt had to admit. "Where did you find such a person? Where have they been hiding in this town?"

Tillie grinned. "Well, right now, she's not hiding. She's sitting right next to you. Meet my new part-time pastry chef." She nodded and Matt followed her gaze and ran smack-dab into a solemn blue one watching him. He swallowed before he choked on the bite of pie he had just taken.

"You? You're the person who did all of this?"

"Don't look so surprised, little brother. She's been making this town happy all week now. And you've been clueless." Tori beamed with laughter.

"Guilty," Ally said. "At first I saw that Tillie was advertising for a new baker with her sign in the window. But the idea that I could do it came to me when you and I were here the day you had me taste her muffins and she mentioned she needed some help. I had time to fill in the mornings before my time with Jillie, and so I had a talk with her that day. I brought a couple of items in for her to taste, and that was it. I meant to say something sooner to you, but we don't really have time to talk when you pick up Jillie. I promise it won't interfere with my time with Jillie in the least."

Matt was still wrapping his head around the news. Ally was full of talent, he was finding out. And to think she hid her light so well. What else could she have not told him? Ally Jones was a woman of mysteries. He just hoped they were all good ones.

Chapter Twelve

ALLY HAD SET the alarm for early the next morning. As in early before the sun rose. She wanted to get a jump on all the baking she needed to do. Not only for Jillie's class project for Fall Fest, but also for the pastry job she had secured at the café. After dropping Jillie at school, she would spend three hours creating magic for the pastries at Tillie's, in the back of that kitchen. As she went about making a list of what she would need, her mind went back over the evening before. It had been quite a dinner in more ways than one.

The fact that Matt had been so surprised by the fact she was not only taking on the class baking project for the annual Fall Fest at the school, but also that she had been hired by Tillie had been out of left field for him. Still, he did manage to congratulate her and wish her well as he had walked her to her car at the end of the evening. They were both well aware of the curious glances sent their way as they had made their way through the café and then outside after the dinner ended. She supposed she was being helpful to the man in some small way. She hoped she was. Matt Parker was a good man. She had thought that from the start, but each day there was something added to cement it in her mind.

In fact, each member of his family that she met seemed

to be of much the same mold. Tori's husband Cade Lockwood was quite handsome and down-to-earth and clearly in love with his wife. Ally had felt some envy watching them together. Sometimes, back in New York, she would see couples walking, holding hands, spending time in Central Park on sunny afternoons while she sat quietly by herself, removed from such things, on a bench feeding the squirrels. She had often imagined what it might be like to have someone in her life, but she would quickly push aside the thought and stop the pity party before it began. She concentrated on what she had: two decent jobs, a safe roof over her head, and Annie who had helped her understand what a home felt like. She would never ask for more.

But then, change had come one day when she'd turned the corner from the subway onto their quiet street and saw the ambulance and a couple of their frantic neighbors, waving and gesturing in a panic when they saw her. She'd dropped her grocery bag and ran to the motionless figure on the stretcher, but the paramedics closed the door as she got there, leaving her heart clamoring and a huge boulder-sized sense of dread pressing her into the pavement. Ally had been informed by a very matter-of-fact nurse that Annie was gone before they reached the hospital.

Ally pushed the memories into the dark hole where she stored them. She'd become good at it; otherwise, she would not have gotten through the days and weeks that followed. Nor would she have come to Destiny's River. And therein lay a whole other world to navigate. The sun was rising as she finally sat down on the front porch to watch the world awaken in the silence that had become such a comfort to her.

Teddy was at her feet, curled up and enjoying the same comforting thoughts, she imagined.

A door opened and she looked at the house across and just one down the street from her porch. A hand rose in her direction and she waved back. That was Mr. Stevens, the local fire marshal, beginning his day at the usual time. He and his wife, Margie—married for thirty-six years, with three adult children and six grandchildren—were a sweet couple who had welcomed her with an apple pie the day after she arrived at Primrose Inn. And that began the morning ritual. It was nice. And the other neighbors on the street would wave in passing and they exchanged 'mornings' or 'nice evenings' as they drove along or walked their dogs along the sidewalk. Ally would rock in the comfy porch rocker and bask in it all. From the largest city to the small country town, she had found something close to what home felt like again. Annie must have known that feeling and held it in her heart for so many years. And that was why she wanted to return for the rest of eternity.

That brought up her meeting with Cade Lockwood. He had been nice and welcoming, and they had chatted about the town and light topics as one usually did upon meeting new people. But then somewhere in the evening, he grew quiet. She'd looked up at one point to find his gaze on her in a very thoughtful way. As though he found something he was trying to work out in his mind. When he realized she had noticed, he smiled again and made a comment about pardoning him but he often had some thoughts, usually about his ranch that he would concentrate on and forget that he might seem odd to others. She had smiled and said she knew the same feeling at times. Yet, that memory had come to her mind again.

The sound of a vehicle pulling into the driveway brought her back to the present. To her surprise, it was a familiar pickup and Matt was driving. Jillie could be seen waving from the passenger's seat. The girl was the first one out of the vehicle when it stopped. And was halfway to the porch before her father could call to her.

"Jillie, you forgot the basket in the back seat."

She stopped and then with a shake of her head, she retraced her steps. "Sorry, Dad. I was in a hurry to hug Teddy." And the dog seemed the same as he had jumped up from his quiet spot and his tail was wagging his own little body as the pair, with a basket in Jillie's arms this time, came up the walk. Ally rose and went to stand beside him.

"Good morning." Matt spoke first. "I had hoped we wouldn't be too early. But we wanted to catch you before breakfast with some of these warm rolls we picked up from Tillie, and she told us that they're the ones you brought for the shop today so that might make us your first customers of the day." His grin was infectious, and it had an effect on her that suddenly made her wish she had dressed in something a bit more stylish than her jeans of many washings and an old blue sweatshirt that she wore if she didn't mind getting flour or other baking ingredients on it. A comfy pair of sneakers completed an outfit that would never be described as alluring. And where had that thought sprung from? Why would she want to look alluring? Then she shut out the answer that her brain had flashed like a neon sign: *Matt.* Stop right there.

"I'm glad you're the first customers. And please come in

and let me get you some coffee or juice, milk maybe…to go with them. That is if you have the time?"

"We have the time," Jillie piped up. "Since you're helping my class and all, we want to help you."

"What my daughter said in a nutshell and meant is, if you would allow us to invade your kitchen, we have come to offer our inexperienced but willing help as your baker assistants or whatever those people are called. We have a free day, and we want to be put to work. That is, if you want us around?"

Yes, indeed. Who wouldn't want them around? She thanked her brain for its unsolicited input, but she took over. "I think that would be great to have such eager help. I won't turn it down. Come in."

She walked ahead of them down the hall to the kitchen that was welcoming and filled with the morning sunshine. "Why don't we begin with those rolls around the kitchen table there in the alcove? Jillie, you know where the small plates are so why don't you set the table with what we need? I'll take the drink orders."

"And I guess I'll bring the biggest appetite to the table?" Matt joked, setting the basket in the center of the table.

"You can make yourself useful in addition to your appetite," Ally responded, setting down the coffee mugs on the cabinet. "You can retrieve the butter dish and the jams from the refrigerator. There is quite a selection of those thanks to Tori's expert stocking of the food in this wonderful kitchen."

It wasn't long before the three of them were seated around the table with its burnt-orange tablecloth with all things fall embroidered on it—acorns, maple leaves, cornucopias. The house had been placed in full Thanksgiving holiday mode when she had arrived. Matt remarked on it as he moved aside the salt and pepper shakers shaped like turkeys to reach the butter dish.

"I'm sorry if this is all a bit much. But Tori always tried to outdo each year's decorations when it came to holidays. She managed to get our grandmother's collection from storage, and she has just added to it with a vengeance. But it was all part of wanting to make this place into our forever home as she called it while we were in foster care."

"Your forever home." Ally smiled. "I like that. And I think all of her decorations are beautiful. They make it even more special. You're lucky to have such a place in your family."

"I suppose we are. Tori had her heart set on finding a home where we would all come and be a family once we left the state's care. And she found Destiny's River and it has turned out to be a good home for all of us. We each took a different route to get here but seems like it just sat waiting until we needed it…coming to it on our own time. The only one not here on a permanent basis is our youngest sibling, Rance. Maybe he'll get here when he decides to settle down. And I'm boring you with our family stuff."

"No, really, I enjoy hearing about family histories and things like that."

"You probably have your own, also." It was a kind prompt for sharing, she was sure. Ally shook her head. "Not really. My family was a bit different from others. But I think it's time we get started on that baking. I know you don't want to spend an entire Saturday on such a thing." She stood up and began clearing their empty glasses. Jillie stood and followed her example. Matt let the subject drop and soon Ally was handing them each an apron from the pantry.

"I found these, and I think they're great. And what a coincidence, they have your names on them," she said with a grin as she handed a pink and white one with ruffled trim to Jillie, and a navy and white checked one to Matt.

"Another of Tori's ideas. She had these done up for when we cook out or whatever over here in the spring and summer. I don't think she would mind in the least if you used hers."

"Dad, we need to get Ally an apron of her own, too."

Matt looked at his daughter and Ally was about to say something when he spoke.

"That's a good idea. We'll have to do that." Why hadn't he played it off and rerouted the child's thinking so that she didn't express her ideas before he spoke? It was a nice idea but then again, she wouldn't be here long enough to ever wear it. That dimmed the moment until he spoke again.

"Ready when you are, Chef. How hard can it be to bust out a few cookies?"

☆

ALLY HAD TO fight back several smiles and bite off a few laughs over the next three hours. The sheriff had found out how hard a 'few cookies' could really turn out to be. For the first batch she had given him simple instructions to follow, but they'd ended up being very crispy instead of the soft, chewy morsels they were supposed to turn into. In fact, crispy was a compliment to the blackened misshaped blobs on the cookie sheet. Whereas Jillie's were coming along nicely, the sheriff gave it a good second try.

"Perhaps instead of salt, you use the sugar instead?" Ally gave her diplomatic assessment as Jillie spit out her bite of cookie from his second batch into the garbage.

"Why don't I mix the batter and the doughs, you place them on the pans and roll out the dough on the others for me? We'll have an assembly line."

Matt looked at her, then he looked down at his apron. "Why is it that you stay so pristine as you cook and even Jillie only has a little patch of flour and a butter swipe on her apron? Whereas I'm hard-pressed to find a spot that isn't covered with some ingredient on my apron. It looks like I rolled myself in the flour instead of the dough."

"Well," Ally considered, her words meant to be constructive, "they say that the mark of a truly great chef in the making, is that he really looks like he gets into his food. That would be apt in your case."

Jillie burst out laughing. Ally bit the inside of her cheek to hold back. Matt looked at them both.

"You both would crack the first minute in an interrogation—if it took that long. Nice try, but I think the saying goes that when a chef is larger in size it means that the food is good enough for even him to eat. Or some such notion. But I appreciate the effort to spare my feelings."

"Good idea that you become my sous chef in the baking department," Ally capitulated.

"Which is a fancy way of saying, Dad," Jillie had to add, "that you get to be on sink duty."

"That I can do."

Ally shook her head. "That comes after you take the cookie cutters and make four dozen turkeys and four dozen maple leaves out of this sugar cookie dough I have waiting right here. Then I'll keep an eye on it in the ovens and begin on the pastry dough recipe to give to Tillie for the rolls for Sunday at the café while you get started on the dirty pans. Sounds like a good plan."

The phone rang and he smiled. "Saved by the bell—if I'm needed in my office." His conversation was short and sweet.

"Let me guess, Dad, you have to go to the office."

"Nope." Matt shook his head and dropped the cell back into his shirt pocket. "You, Miss Smarty-Pants, are going with your aunt, who is on her way to pick you up, to go have the fitting at Verna's shop for your costume for the play. Miss Verna needs to move your appointment up and Aunt Tori is taking you since she knows I'm elbow-deep in flour."

After a moment of thinking, he asked, "How did she know that?"

"Guess she knows you pretty well and made an educated guess when you mentioned you were helping make cookies," Ally replied with a simple smile.

Jillian laughed, while untying her apron. "She got you on that one, Dad."

"You need to wait on the porch for your aunt, so she doesn't have to get out of the car in her condition."

"Yes, sir. Bye and thanks a bunch for doing the cookies and all," Jillie said and gave Ally a quick hug before she headed down the hall and outside.

"I can't believe my daughter did that," Matt said with a shake of his head.

"I'm sorry." Ally felt unsure what to say. "She's just a sweet girl and she likes to hug people and—"

"I can't believe that she totally skipped me. What about my hug? Just because I'm standing here in a mess being the butt of jokes for my cookie-making skills and all. It has nothing to do with her hugging you."

Ally felt more at ease. She gave him a rueful smile. "I see. It's the male ego thing."

He gave her a long look then walked around the corner of the wide island work area. She looked at him with a silent question. His hand rose and one fast finger slid down her nose, leaving a white line of flour in its wake. "You look better sharing in some of the messiness."

Ally was at first speechless. Then something overtook her. She raised her hand and with two fingers planted a trail of flour mixed with a bit of cookie dough across his cheek. Then there was a dawning sensation of what she had just done…about the same time his gaze darkened to jade and dropped to her mouth. Was there any air in the room? Would he? He wouldn't dare…or would he? And then she had her answer when his lips brushed hers…once. Then twice. And then he stepped back. Perhaps just as shocked as she was? They both looked at each other in silence.

"You had some cookie dough on the corner of your mouth."

"Thank you." Then there she went again…the little devil inside herself that couldn't stay hidden. She took a step and went up on tiptoe and her lips brushed his cheek. Then she stepped back. "Sorry, but you had some dough on your cheek."

A small gleam appeared in his eyes and a corner of his mouth lifted at some unknown thought. "Maybe we better just use paper towels next time…or the rest of the dough might get used up." Then he winked and she felt her cheeks grow too warm.

The timer on the oven went off like a loud clanging church bell in her brain's way of thinking. Ally jumped back and grabbed for a potholder. "Must save the cookies."

That sounded ridiculous to her the moment the words left her mouth. She was not going to give him the satisfaction of looking at him anytime soon. So, she kept busy on the other side of the kitchen. He did the same.

What had she gotten herself into by a sudden little mischievous prank? She knew better. Or did she?

Chapter Thirteen

"WELL, TILLIE, IS this your latest hired employee? I heard you found someone who got stuck here after almost running over our poor little Jillie Parker. Her father must be SOOO furious. The poor man. I'm surprised she isn't in one of his jail cells."

Ally's back was to the counter when the words were spoken but before she could turn around, Tillie was putting the speaker straight.

"No. Ally is a baking marvel and absolutely a godsend. And your information source is erroneous as usual. If anything, she took action that saved Jillie from any harm and ended up being the one in the hospital. We're all surprised Matt Parker was able to keep from giving her a medal on the courthouse steps for her bravery. Ally Jones, meet Frannie Willis, just recently back from a few months in Dallas."

Ally was a quick study of people most of the time. She was able to realize as she turned to the counter that by Tillie's tone and body language, this was not one of her most endearing customers…to say the least. The woman sat on the barstool at the counter as though she might be perched on either an ivory throne or a stack of rotten garbage—her attitude and bearing could go either way. Her hair was piled on top of her head in some type of hairstyle that was either done by a novice in a beauty school or someone fleeing from a windstorm. She wasn't certain if the woman was attempting to allow her dark roots to grow out or thought the blonde color from the bottle was enough to cover them all. But the makeup was a bit much for the morning hour, or any hour of day at that.

Was her drawl that natural or was she trying to fake it? Ally had a feeling that there wasn't much on the person in front of her that would be the genuine article.

"It's Francesca—how many times must I correct you?"

Before Tillie could shoot back with whatever was on the tip of her tongue at the woman's response, Ally stepped into the breach. She smiled at the woman who instantly responded with a frown.

"Francesca is a lovely name. And it's a pleasure to meet another citizen of Destiny's River. You're lucky to live in such a beautiful place with so many lovely people."

"I don't live here in this small town all the time. I prefer our house in Dallas. I can see you're a small-town girl."

"I only wish I were. I come from New York City. It truly is the city that never sleeps…Broadway, The Met, Manhattan…so much to do and on the go constantly. It gets boring after a few years."

The woman wasn't quite sure which way to respond but the bell above the door of the café signaled another patron had entered. This one elicited a squeal of pleasure from the woman who left her throne and immediately threw her arms around the man's neck and planted a kiss on him in a movement that clearly caught him off guard. His arms went up and extricated hers from his neck and put some space between them.

"You're back in town," he said, darting a quick glance in the direction of Ally and Tillie. "What a surprise, Frannie."

"Francesca," the woman corrected, and Ally stifled a smile when she could visualize a stomp of her foot going along with her correction of the sheriff.

"You'll always be just Frannie to those of us who have known you a while," he said and moved toward the counter.

"I've just met the latest visitor to our town," she continued, following behind him and slipping onto the stool next to his. "She was telling me how exciting the life is in New York City."

Ally wanted to correct her, but Tillie was ahead.

"You still have that problem with your hearing, Frannie? Ally said she loved this small town, and New York was just too busy all the time. Maybe you should get your ears checked?"

Ally had to focus on an object at the end of the bar in order to keep from breaking out in a laugh at how Tillie was handling the woman and her twisting of truths. She could watch that go on all day. But she had other places to be.

"I'm sorry but I've got to run. I have a meeting at the school for the Fall Fest committee."

"I have the same one. I saw your car over here and came in to see if you wanted to ride over together. Then I can bring you back and we can discuss the fest lists I'm sure we're going to have on the way there." He was already on his feet and the woman beside him was not liking how things were turning out.

"That's a plan," Ally agreed. "And Jillie has that sleepover this evening so you and I can have dinner at my house."

"That's my girl," Matt said with a wide smile. "I do like your planning."

"Your girl?" That had Frannie's attention.

"Well, you certainly heard that without a problem," Tillie threw in, but didn't stop there. "You've been gone a while. Things have changed for our sheriff. Goodbye bachelorhood. The whole town is happy for him. You two are going to be late."

She gave them the cue and they didn't hesitate. Although Ally would have enjoyed staying a bit longer to bask in the look of shock and anger that brought out the wrinkles despite Frannie's obvious facelifts. Both she and Matt were out the door and in his vehicle in minutes. Then as they turned the corner, both couldn't help it any longer. They burst out laughing.

"What got into Tillie?"

"I have no idea, but I'm glad it did," he responded to her question. "It was long overdue in Tillie's mind, I guess. She's like the rest of us…trying to ignore Frannie's rudeness and tune her out."

"She didn't tune her out today," Ally said. "I hope it wasn't on my account. I've come across some rude people where I come from. You get to where they just become background noise, and you put on your headphones and tune them out."

"Well, it has become increasingly difficult to do that. Seems she is dead set on my being husband number two…or is it three?"

"Oh, my heavens," Ally said, shaking her head. "You

have been lucky to escape this long."

"It was thanks to you and Tillie. We do seem to be making a good team. Thanks, by the way."

"Thanks?"

"For going along with Tori's scheme to give me some breathing space from the single women in this town. Although most of them seemed to take a hint early on. But then Frannie has always been that lone wolf not heeding any warnings. She writes her own rules."

"I've seen her type before. And with her broken marriages, I guess it does add up to her being a lonely and bitter person."

"Are you a psychologist?"

"No…I've just seen enough and heard enough among the rich friends of my former employer. I sat with her kids as one of my jobs. You pick up a lot of things when those bored ladies get to talking. Sad really."

"You have a soft and empathetic heart. That's rare these days."

"I won't deny it. I prefer that to having a hard heart and being unhappy. Guess Annie rubbed off on me more than I know."

"From what you've told me about her, I've come to think she was more of a surrogate mother to you than good friend."

"I suppose that may be true. I know I miss her wisdom. I do hope she knows I'm trying to carry out her wishes to come back to Destiny's River." Then she corrected herself. "To come back for her. She wanted me to experience it."

"Well, I hope you are. And you are about to go into this

school and experience a whole bunch of it." He laughed, parking the vehicle. As he came around to open her door, she drew in her breath. She had almost slipped up with him. Annie had wanted her last wish to be kept a secret and that was what Ally was doing her best to accomplish.

☆

"HOW WAS THE meeting?" Tori asked a couple of hours later when she called to check in with Matt. "How did people respond to Ally?"

"You don't need to worry about Ally. She handled herself like she was used to disorganization and too many ideas and curious stares and you name it. She ended up moving the discussion where it needed to focus, a lot like you would have, and the agenda was on track, and we had responsibilities divided out before people knew what was going on. And they left smiling and inviting Ally to various other activities. She was a hit…by being herself."

"Do I sense a bit of pride in your tone? And I heard about the Frannie incident, too. Good job both of you!"

"Frannie? How did you…"

"Tillie and the diners in the café. Bless their hearts." She laughed and Matt had to join in.

"Too true. If I didn't know better, I'd say Ally was a lifelong resident of Destiny's River. Maybe it'll grow on her."

Tori was smiling big time but he couldn't see that. Cade could as he lay beside her in their big bed, reading while she caught up with her brother. He shook his head and went back to his book. "Sounds like *she's* growing on you, too."

"Okay, knock that off. Stick to reality. She's here until her car is repaired and she's paid me back for fixing the damage on it. She is one stubborn woman…a lot like you. But her plan is to move on and you need to remember that."

"Plans change. And, whether you want to admit it or not, Ally Jones is different. And both you and Jillie are different than before she came. There's a spark in your lives and she put it there. Just don't go putting it out with your hardheadedness. Take a chance. She leaves and you didn't try, then you'll always regret it."

"I hear you. Now get some sleep and concentrate on bringing that nephew or niece of mine into this world and stop wasting time."

Matt still had a smile on his face after the conversation ended. He took his glass of iced tea out on the patio. The stars were huge, and the night air had chilled a bit. Autumn had arrived. Soon it would be Thanksgiving. Then Christmas and all the festivities in the town would only grow more. Ally would enjoy the Fall Fest. And the tree lighting and parade…and then there was the Christmas Ball. And New Year's Eve and… He stopped. All those things he had associated Ally as part being of. That surprised him. He hadn't done that…well since Casey had been with them. What would Casey think of Ally? He had a strange feeling that she would really have liked having her as a friend. They were a lot alike. But Ally might have more spark in her. Not as quiet as Casey. But then Ally came from a different life in one of the biggest cities in the world. Casey had been a farm girl when he met her and then a small-town girl when they married. She had died a few hours after Jillie had been born.

She would forever be frozen in time as she was then.

And she had wanted him to promise to marry and find a good mother for their daughter and wife for himself. She was as unselfish as Ally for certain. He had promised, but it hadn't been all that easy. He couldn't marry if there wasn't love involved and no woman had caused that particular spark to ignite. *Until*...and that word's appearance in his mind caused him to regroup his thoughts. Love at first sight? No way. Love at second or third? Now that was getting ridiculous. But Ally was not the usual type of woman he had come across. There was something. Maybe his sister was right...*again*. Give it a chance. There was time. She wasn't gone yet.

A few minutes later, he stood in that same spot watching the stars, but this time he dialed a number in his cell phone. It was answered on the third ring.

"Hi, I hope it's not too late to call," he said.

"No," she replied with a soft laugh. "Teddy and I were just having a discussion about his hurrying up outside and getting back into the warm house."

"Welcome to a foretaste of a Texas fall. It is chilly tonight. Tomorrow you could be turning your AC back on high. Then we could have snowflakes the next day. As they say, if you don't like Texas weather, just give it a few minutes. It'll show you."

"I shall remember that sage advice and keep my summer clothing handy, too."

There was a slight pause, and he took a deep breath and plunged forward. "The reason I called was to invite you to dinner tomorrow. I should have done it before now. It's to thank you for being so great about Jillie and taking care of her and going so far as to be involved in the Fall Fest and all. You have gone far above what you need to do. The least I can do is grill you one of my amazing steaks."

"Amazing?"

"That's the word used most often when I grill for family and friends. You will be amazed."

"I warn you, it takes a lot to amaze me."

"How do you like your steak? Medium well? That is great because…"

"Well done."

There was a beat or two. "Well done? As in no pink at all?"

"No pink at all. I've only had one amazing steak cooked well done the right way…cooked through, no pink, and juicy. That's a tall order for most chefs."

"Well…I can do that. One well-done perfectly juicy steak tomorrow at six."

"I'll be there. I can hardly wait to taste the amazing steak."

Matt looked at his phone after the call ended. Maybe he could cancel in the morning. Pressing business out of town. With luck she would forget his boast about his steak prowess. The only time he had attempted a well-done steak it had been too tough to chew let alone too dry, and the steak knife had to be sharpened again. That's what he got for trying to impress and being cute and basically asking a girl on a date. Not an actual date…but close. And he looked at his watch.

He would need time to get a crash course from his brother-in-law and maybe even Tillie.

He was not about to fail. But then again…he could always leave town on an emergency.

Chapter Fourteen

"I THOUGHT YOU were joking," Tillie said as she stood on the porch behind the café early next afternoon and watched in amusement as Carl, her main cook, went over the intricacies of cooking a well-done steak.

"I don't joke about cooking," Matt said, trying to remember every word his teacher spoke.

"Why don't you just let Carl grill you a steak and be done with it?"

"It's not the same thing," Matt answered trying to get the subject closed.

"Why not?"

Carl spoke up next time. "Geez, Tillie, give the guy a break. He's going to this much trouble to learn what it takes years to perfect and do it in just hours… It means there is a special woman involved somehow."

Tillie's eyes lit up. "Ally? You're cooking Ally a special meal? How romantic. Why steak?"

"Because I said I was an amazing griller of steaks. Little did I know that she eats hers well done to the point of charcoal if need be."

"Oh wow," Tillie said, shaking her head. "You're in big trouble. Unless you just give her charcoal and be done with it."

"You are no help."

That was much the same help he received from his daughter when he went through the same conversation later that evening just before Ally was set to arrive. It did little for his confidence.

"Hello," Ally said following Jillie out onto the patio where the grill was set. "It smells delicious."

"Thanks. You look very nice by the way. Jillie, why don't you see what Ally will drink and get it for her?"

Jillie left with her request for iced tea and his for the same. "I'm glad you could come over and let us try to…"

Jillie ran from the house. "Dad, Uncle Cade called, and your phone was on the kitchen cabinet. They're on their way to the hospital. We need to go. Hurry!"

Ally saw his hesitation. She stood. "Why don't you go and I can stay with Jillie so you don't have…"

"No, Aunt Tori said I could come whenever it happened. Right, Dad?"

"Yes, she did."

"I'm sorry, I didn't realize. You both go and we'll do this some other time."

"Her labor might be a long one and, Jillie, you have school tomorrow so how about, if Ally doesn't mind, she could follow us in her car and if we see it's going to be a long night, then she can bring you back home." He looked at Ally and she nodded.

"She can even stay with me overnight if needed. So, I suggest you turn off the grill and we get moving."

Fifteen minutes later, the trio arrived in the waiting room. Cade was standing talking to the doctor. He saw them and came over. "I'm about to go back and stay with her. She's only about halfway and in pain of course. So far, the baby is doing good. I'll come out when I can, or the nurse will let you know what's going on. Thanks for being here, all of you," and he included Ally in his thankful glance. He left them to make themselves as comfortable as one could in a maternity waiting room. One hour turned into two and then three. Jillie had spent her excited energy and was dozing off curled into one of the couches. Ally had gone and found the cafeteria and came back with soft drinks and some sandwiches.

"This isn't quite the meal I had planned for this evening. Sorry about that." Matt shook his head and offered her a bag of potato chips.

Ally grinned and took the bag. "This is still a good evening. Besides, I love picnics."

"This isn't exactly my idea of a great location for a picnic." He grinned, looking around at the small waiting room area. The last few people had been called for the arrival of their babies, but they were still waiting. His smile faded a bit. Ally noted it.

"I can't help thinking that there's something on your mind. It might be none of my business, but is there some reason you might be worried about Tori's labor?"

"You're very sensitive to others' moods," he noted. "Worried? I know my sister is tough. And her doctor is the best. But memories can intrude when they're least expected."

"Memories as in what happened to your wife?"

"I try to keep things upbeat around Jillie. But I guess it's inevitable that those memories of being in this same hospital, waiting for a birth to happen—they're bound to find their way into my brain."

Ally laid a hand on his as it rested on his knee. "It's only human. But you're right in what you said about Tori. I have a feeling that she will do this beautifully just as she does everything else for her family and the people of this town. You Parkers are a tough group."

"This is certainly not how I wanted tonight to go…good food, good company…and you get this instead."

"Sure, a nice location with good scenery is great, but it's the people, the company, that matter the most. And you gave me a rain check on that steak."

"I would have to agree with that one. Here's to great company and a rain check for the next one."

"Agreed. Poor Jillie." Ally looked at the sleeping child. "Perhaps I should take her home? I'll get her to school in the morning and do the regular after-school stuff with her."

"She'll be really upset if she misses her cousin's entrance. But she is too tired. If anything happens, I'll stop by your house and let her know. The nurse did say it could be another few hours."

"Don't worry about a thing. And Tori will be fine. She is a tough lady—as you know."

He carried Jillie outside in his arms. She was struggling to wake up but losing the battle. He placed her in the seat and buckled her in. Then he made sure Ally was settled inside. Her window was down, and he placed palms on the doorframe. His tone was low and full of sincerity.

"Thanks for being such a good sport about all of this to-night. It didn't go like I had hoped with the dinner and all, but it means a lot that you understood."

"You and your family have welcomed me and made me feel like part of this family and town in so many ways. Annie was right about this place and the people. So, there's no need to thank me."

Then Matt did something that felt right. He leaned in and placed a kiss on her lips, and they met his in unison. The kiss was brief, but it lasted far beyond that moment. It wasn't just a thank you. It was wrapped in a promise of much more still to be named. But for the moment, it was everything.

No more words were spoken, and he stood for a few moments watching the red taillights grow dimmer in the distance until they were not visible. Hands in pockets, he re-entered the building with purpose in his steps and a hope in his heart that had been missing for a very long time.

An hour later the swinging doors opened, and a tired but exuberant Cade strode out, seeming to be walking on air. Matt jumped up and the men embraced without speaking. Then the dam broke and laughter mixed with some manly tears.

"She's amazing."

Matt wasn't sure who was amazing, so he had to ask. "Which she? Tori or…?"

"Tori! The determination and the strength—she's just incredible."

"So, what about the reason we're here? Get to it, man. The baby!"

"Perfect!" Cade beamed. "Seven pounds, eight ounces, twenty-two inches long, all fingers and toes, and got a great set of lungs."

"And..." Matt prompted. "What is it?"

"Oh...that's right. I forgot to tell you."

"I swear you're doing this on purpose... Spit it out!"

The man's smile broadened as did his chest. "A boy. A son. I have a son. Come see him." Cade was already halfway through the doors when Matt got over the shock of surprise and fell in line behind him. Tori was in the room just down the hall and Cade held the door open for Matt to enter.

Tori looked great with a huge smile on her face and a little bundle wrapped in a blue blanket in her arms. "It's time for you to meet your uncle Matt." She adjusted the fold around the newborn's face and Matt approached slowly, trying to focus. For some odd reason there seemed to be some moisture crowding his vision.

"Oh my, Tori. He is amazing." Matt laid his finger on top of the blanket fold to better see his new nephew's face. It was claimed as if on cue, by a little fist that held on to it. And that little fist had reached right into his heart and staked their claim.

"This is Joseph Caden Lockwood. And this is your uncle Matt, and he will always watch out for you, too. Just like Momma and Daddy, will."

"Hey, little man. What a grip. You're going to be a baseball player."

"A quarterback," his dad corrected.

"A little boy with a mind of his own to choose for himself, gentlemen," Tori corrected, already being the mother hen.

"He will be a little boy with awesome parents," Matt added. "And a cousin who gave it up and crashed about an hour ago. Ally took her home to bed. But she'll be here bright and early, I'm sure."

"Speaking of bed—" the nurse stood just inside the door "—it's time this youngster and his mom got some rest."

Matt met his sister's gaze. "She's right. You won't get much sleep for the next eighteen years or so. If your raising of us three is any indication."

"What do you mean eighteen? I keep an eye open for you three… Always will."

Matt leaned over and placed a kiss on her forehead. He needed to make his exit before the darn moisture became blinding. "See you in the morning, sis." He gently squeezed the little fist that had let go of his finger. "Take care of Mom, Joey. Big job you have ahead of you." He turned to Cade and shook his hand. "And you have the watch over them. Congrats, Dad."

Matt dialed Ally's number as soon as he was in his vehicle. She answered on the second ring. Her voice was lowered but sounded good to him even at a distance.

"It's a boy. Perfect and so is Mom. Dad looks a little shaky," he said with a laugh, "but they're all settling in for sleep. Is Jillie awake?"

"No, she was out like a light almost before her head hit the pillow. That is great news—and congratulations, Uncle Matt."

"Thanks. I'm very happy for us all."

"If you want, how about you let Jillie sleep here and then I'll meet you at the hospital early in the morning so she can see the baby before she goes to class or else she won't be able to concentrate much until she does get to see him."

"How did you know that's what I was going to suggest? It makes sense if you're sure it's okay?"

"Well, great minds think alike sometimes." She laughed. "And that way you can get home and get some sleep and so can she. She can see the baby before her first class at nine."

"Sounds like a plan. I'll see you at the hospital about eight?"

"Okay, sounds good. And Ally?"

"Yes?"

"Thanks again. For knowing what I was thinking and for being you and just…everything."

"Get some sleep, Sheriff. See you tomorrow."

☆

IT TOOK ALLY a little while to calm her brain. She lay in the dark. Teddy had moved himself into the bedroom across the hall and was probably not asleep on the floor where Ally had permitted but on the bed with Jillie. And she smiled at that.

In a perfect world, in her dreams, she had often thought about such things. A quiet home, those she loved and who loved her, asleep and all was well and safe. That dream had gotten her through many a long night…even spilling into her waking hours. But that was all it had been…a dream. Soon to evaporate into reality.

Just like this all would one day. It was coming. Another month or so, and she would have enough saved to pay back Matt for all his generosity. And hopefully the closing on the apartment would be done and then she and Teddy would start off. Where? That was the question that kept nagging at her. Once she had taken care of Annie's wish and settled her debts, then they would be free. North? Too cold. East…been there, too many people. West…empty space for sure, hot. South…stay in Texas? Find a small town like Destiny's River to make their home?

One step, one day at a time, little one. Words Annie had spoken to her often. She needed to remember that mantra more each day. Because something was happening. She wished for Annie's words of wisdom more than ever. The people in Destiny's River were becoming too close to her heart. That meant they would be harder to leave…and more so to forget. But she should be grateful. They had shown her a wonderful reality even for a short time. Some of her dreams could come true… That life was out there. She just had to find it for herself. *What about Matt Parker?*

That voice was becoming louder than the rest. It would not go away as easily as the others. And the kiss at the hospital…had to be kept in perspective. It was a thank you. *Don't read more into it.* Matt was sincerely glad for her help. She knew that. And it just made her want to help him, and Jillie, and Tori and all the others she had met in Destiny's River. Because that is what you did when you cared. And that was the word she would not allow to change. Because there was another word that was just a whisper away waiting to take its place. She couldn't allow anything like love to enter into her thinking or feeling. It hurt too much when it went away.

In a perfect world, she might dream of staying in Destiny's River. She would always be part of the Parker family. And they would share so many happy things together in

Primrose Inn. *And who do you think you are?* That question would pop up and bring her back to reality. Dreams faded when eyes opened. Some people belonged and some did not.

She'd learned that as a child. And she kept on learning that lesson as a homeless teen. She had allowed it in when Annie had given her a home and care and love. But that love left when she died. It was just too painful to have that emotion. She fought to keep that wall intact. Reality was the sword used to protect it. *Reality.*

☆

"WHAT'S HIS NAME? How big is he? I kinda hoped for a girl and all, but that's okay. I can still teach him things." Jillie was chattering a mile a minute in the car. And she practically raced from the parking lot to the front doors of the hospital. She shifted her weight from one foot to the other as she waited for Ally to catch up before entering the lobby.

Matt pulled into the parking lot just as Ally reached the front door. She made Jillie wait for her father to join them. He came up to them smiling and Ally felt that tug in the center of her chest that was beginning to take root if she wasn't careful.

"Good morning, beautiful ladies. Fine morning, isn't it?" His gaze swept them both but lingered a bit longer on hers. Or was it her dream bumping aside reality?

"Hurry, Dad, let's go inside." She pushed through the door, and they were left to follow. A couple minutes more and Jillie was transfixed next to Cade, who was already watching over his son being tended to by one of the nurses.

"Congratulations. How is the new dad holding up?" Ally greeted Cade who looked a little tired but a whole lot of happy.

"I still can't quite believe he's ours and will come home with us tomorrow. Tori went through so much to bring him into this world, and she looks like she's ready to jump out of bed and get to the office on time. You women are tougher than us men, that's for sure," Cade said, and then his smile faded as his gaze noted her hand on his arm. But Jillie claimed his attention then and his grin returned. Ally hoped she hadn't been too forward in her greeting, but perhaps he was a man operating on little sleep.

"Tori would like you all to come by the house tomorrow evening. Dinner will be pot roast and whatever else Mrs. James has planned. About six thirty sound okay?"

"Good with us." Matt spoke up and then looked at Ally. "But you and Jillie will be coming from play rehearsal?"

"We can make it by then." Ally had hoped for an invitation to the Lockwood Ranch since she had heard so much about it and the springs that had brought Tori and Cade together in the first place. She was as interested in a good romance story as the next person and Tillie had told her bits and pieces of it one day at the café.

"We can talk more about it when I pick up Jillie," Matt said.

"And I do have to run right now. I have to finish the pastry order over at the café for Tillie."

"Have a good day and see you later," Ally said. "Please give Tori my best and tell her I can't wait to see her tomorrow," she told Cade, who had watched the interchange between her and Matt with interest.

Ally left the hospital and began her day. Her thoughts stayed with Matt and Jillie and their happiness in welcoming a new member of their family. That's what families did. They were blessed to have that. And Cade and Tori—now parents—had a little one to watch grow up and the circle would grow and continue. A circle she envied. Maybe someday? Someday she might be part of such a circle. She had often dreamed of such a family circle…through foster homes and even finding a home with Annie. But each time, the dream always ended. So, *dream on*. She thanked her brain for reminding her.

Chapter Fifteen

"THE PLAY IS in just four days," Jillie stressed. "Some people don't know their lines—and what if I forget the words of the song? I could ruin it all."

Matt glanced in the rearview mirror at his daughter. He shook his head. "I know that you'll be great. And that is not just your dad talking," he added before she could deliver her usual response when he said such things. "You know your lines because you have rehearsed them over and over. You know the stanza of the song you're doing as a solo part, because you sing it enough around the house and at Ally's, and you are prepared just like you have been for all the other plays and choir concerts you've done."

"But something could still go wrong," Jillie responded.

"And there is something you can remember about that." Ally spoke up from the front passenger seat, half turning to speak with the worried child. "No one in the audience knows what the play is about. They don't know what your lines are, and they don't know the song. Even if anyone makes a mistake on that stage, no one in the audience will be any the wiser and they will enjoy whatever the performance is, because they know you and your classmates are doing your very best. So, if you and your classmates will continue to do that, plus try to enjoy it at the same time, your audience will do the same."

Jillie shot her a smile. "That's true. I never thought of it like that."

Ally turned back to face front and caught Matt's smile of thanks for what she had done for Jillie's mood. She smiled back and the rest of the ride to the Lockwood Ranch was enjoyable. They passed through the gates and Ally became immersed in the fields where horses—many with foals at their sides—grazed. Tall trees followed a creek that ran a few yards from the roadway and then they climbed through the trees, and she could see surrounding hills that enclosed a field of green where a beautiful sprawling house sat in the middle. In the distance she could see barns down a side road.

"This is beautiful," she said, as they parked in the circular driveway. "It is something out of one of those television shows about Texans and ranches."

"But not nearly so dramatic, I hope." Matt grinned as he opened the door for her and Jillie scrambled out of the back seat. He reached onto the floorboard and withdrew the bouquet of flowers they had brought for Tori. Ally held a wrapped package—she had managed to shop for and found a couple of cute little boy infant outfits that she thought Tori would like.

The front door opened, and Cade stood with a welcoming smile. "Come on in. Tori is in the living room with Joey, who had his dinner and is ready to receive his guests."

For the next few minutes everyone made baby talk and smiled and laughed. Tori loved her flowers, and she fell in love with the little denim outfits that Ally had found. "Joseph will wear these when he goes to the play and the Fall

Fest next Saturday."

Cade shook his head. "If he goes—he might want to stay home a little longer."

Tori gave a certain smile to her husband. "He will be just fine. The doctor said so. We will go to see Jillie's play and make a quick circle through the festival and then head home. All depending of course on Joseph being in a good mood." They all laughed.

"I hope you like the play, Aunt Tori. And the booths are really cool, and our pastry booth is the most awesome because Ally is the best baker ever and the whole town loves her cooking."

"Really? Seems like I have heard that a time or two around town myself," Tori responded. "My husband is particularly fond of your pecan fudge bars."

"I do enjoy those," Cade admitted with a grin.

"Speaking of food, Mrs. James is motioning for us. Let's not keep her good food waiting."

The dinner was wonderful. The conversation even better. Joey fell asleep in his mother's arms and Cade took him from her and quietly moved toward the stairs. He glanced back and nodded to Ally to her surprise. "Would you like the fifty-cent tour of the house while I take him to the nursery?"

Ally wasn't going to turn such an offer down. She wanted to see more of the beautiful home with its winding grand staircase lined with portraits of Lockwoods, she surmised, and overseen by a beautiful chandelier of polished wood and lanterns. The nursery was a child's delight. Joey was going to enjoy it as he got older, but for the time being, his dad laid him gently inside the crib and then set the monitor so they could hear his slightest sound. They tiptoed out. Once in the hallway, Ally was free to look at the photos and Cade named a few of them.

They were almost to the bottom of the stairs when he hesitated in front of an oval portrait of a man in a cowboy hat and clothing. He was seated in a chair and his hands rested one on each knee.

"This is my grandfather. He raised me and my sister. She was attracted to the bright lights and I wasn't, so I became his shadow and he taught me everything I know."

Ally noted the resemblance in the men. And then she noted something that made her go cold down her back. She didn't move or show surprise, but her gaze was riveted on his hand as it rested on his knee, his ring froze in her brain. It was like the one she wore, sometimes on a chain around her neck and sometimes on the middle finger of her right hand. But usually, it was on a chain as she was afraid of losing the one thing that made her feel close to Annie. Annie had never taken off the necklace as long as she had known her. And when she died, Mr. Jacobs had handed it to Ally with her love. How could it be just like the one she had?

Cade stood close and could feel him watching her. What was it all about? She pulled the ring up from beneath her sweater on the chain that secured it. Her gaze met his steady one.

"I noticed it that first night at dinner at the café. I was wondering if that has something to do with what really brought you here to our town. You seem shocked."

"I don't understand how they are so similar."

"They aren't similar. The one on his hand was given over

to the woman he loved all his life. But lost. That woman was not my grandmother, the woman he married. How did you come across it, Ally Jones?"

Ally had difficulty still trying to fit the pieces. "I was given this ring when someone very dear to me died and she left it to me. With specific instructions that baffled me at first but now seem to be becoming clearer."

"I think we need to talk about this in more detail. And I don't want to do it in front of the others until we know the whole story. Agreed?"

She nodded. "I think that's wise."

"Then let's smile and join the others," Cade said.

The rest of the evening was a blur as her mind was on the photo and the ring and how they all fit together. She knew she smiled and laughed when appropriate, but she couldn't say what else happened until they were at the front door bidding Tori and Cade thanks and good night.

"I heard your remarks about the horses you saw earlier in the pasture, Ally." Cade spoke up as they stood on the front porch. "Would you like to see some of them up close and personal? We are moving some of them into the barns and such tomorrow. If you have the time, you could come out in the morning and visit."

Ally was caught off guard for a moment, but then she found her voice. "I would love that."

"Couldn't I come, too?" Jillie piped up. "I love the horses."

"You have something to do called school, remember?" Matt reminded her. "Can you find your way out here by yourself? I could bring you, but my morning is booked."

She shook her head. "No worries. When I go to someplace new once, I can find my way there again. And there is a wonderful invention called the GPS." They all laughed.

"It's settled. I'll expect you to join us about ten?"

"That will be wonderful." Ally felt she could have won an award for the performance she went through as she sat in the dark of her front porch, bundled in a warm blanket and robe, thinking back over the evening. No one seemed wiser. Only she and Cade knew the events of the conversation and discovery. Tomorrow would come too slowly she feared. And she feared more what might transpire when she shared what she knew with Cade.

☆

IT HAD BEEN a sleepless night. Ally dressed, including the usual chain with its ring, which she often had seen Annie rub between her fingers absently, her thoughts far away, Ally could tell in those moments. She knew that the woman was in a place that was far better than the present and she often envied her that. They never really spoke about the details, but Ally knew that the ring and a town called Destiny's River was where Annie's heart had remained.

The gate was open as it had been the evening before. She wondered as she had driven out what Cade might have told Tori about the ring, and Ally wondered if she should have shared the information with Matt. Would he be upset in some way that she had not confided in him? But she hadn't thought it would even concern him. Except now, the bits and pieces were falling into place.

Cade was standing in the driveway talking to a man who held the reins of a beautiful horse. She wished she was just there to see the horses and not on the errand she was there for today. But she had vowed to honor Annie's last wish, and she would do it no matter what.

"Good morning, Ally," Cade greeted her as she stepped out of the car. "Ally Jones, this is James Stoddard, he's my equine manager—a fancy name for horse whisperer extraordinaire."

The older man had removed his hat and nodded his welcome. "Fancy name but just a cowboy all the same." He grinned.

"James brought our pride and joy up to meet you," he said taking the reins from the man and drawing the animal closer to Ally. "She loves to have someone stroke her nose, just so," he said, demonstrating, "and she will be your bestie for life."

Ally couldn't believe she was getting to touch such a beautiful creature, and the horse was enjoying it, nudging her hand when it seemed like she might be removing it. Ally obliged with more rubs.

"I love her. What's her name?"

James responded. "Her fancy name is Belle's Enduring Dream. But to the rest of us, she's just Belle."

"What a beautiful Belle you are," Ally whispered and received a gentle nudge of the nose.

"Belle's going to join the rest of her stablemates, but you'll see her again and meet the others." Cade handed over the reins to James.

"Enjoy your time on the ranch, Miss Jones. Hurry back

and see us."

James and Belle headed down the road to the barn area and that left Cade and Ally.

"Thank you for that," she said. "I know that was just the excuse in front of the others last night and I appreciate the fact I did get to meet such a magnificent creature."

"Well, an excuse or not, Matt told me earlier that you expressed a love for animals and horses, and he wanted to bring you out to ride some weekend. So, we might as well get you used to the place and check out the riding stock we have. But first, let's take a ride in my Jeep over here. I want to show you the springs."

"Does Tori know why I came out today?" She ventured that question as they left the ranch house behind and headed toward a distant hill.

"My wife and I don't keep things from each other. I filled her in this morning, and she knows we need to talk. And you need to know that nothing we talked about leaves the three of us. Not until and unless you decide. I'm sure you still have questions and so do I."

"I know it must have been a shock to see the ring that belonged to your grandfather in the possession of a stranger. I never expected to see it in a photo of someone other than Annie."

They had climbed along a narrow road to the summit of a hill and stopped. Ally followed Cade to where a few trees stood grouped around a rock-edged pool of water that disappeared into a stream that emptied over the side of the hill.

"What a beautiful spot," she murmured, her gaze taking

in the vast view from the hilltop. The valley lay stretched below them and in the far distance she saw a church steeple that she thought might be the one in Destiny's River. "I can just imagine this place when the trees are full and green, and the grass is growing out from the winter. I would come here often if this was mine."

"Well, this is the spot where I believe that my grandfather would meet your Annie and the spot where he proposed to her and gave her the ring."

Cade's words surprised Ally. And the fact she was standing where Annie had stood in her happiest moments so long ago, made moisture threaten her eyes.

"How do you know that?"

"My grandfather brought me up here toward the end of his days and shared a good deal with me. Until that time, I had no idea that my grandmother had not been the love of his life. Granted she had died when I was still a teenager, and I believed them to be as happy as I thought most married people were...but that had not been the case. He told me how he met this beautiful girl with the eyes of a doe and hair that was long and raven's-wing black. And how he had fallen in love at first sight. But her family was poor...and while she loved him in return, she knew that his family would expect better. And they did. My great-grandfather was vehemently set on my grandfather marrying the daughter of another big rancher and adding even more land to the Lockwood brand.

"It sounds archaic to say such things, but those patriarchal practices existed then and still do today in some instances. According to my grandfather, a note was left at their tree...which I will show you in a moment...she had left town and begged him not to follow. She had returned the ring. But he hired a detective a couple years later and he found where she had gone and then money changed hands, and the ring was delivered by special courier to Annie—and that was that. My grandfather did what was expected and married the rancher's daughter. He had a son who had me and my sister and here we are."

"How very sad. To think how things might have been for them had it not been for greed coming first. And I don't mean to offend you. But I know that Annie never once stopped loving your grandfather. She never spoke of him to me except to say that the love of her life was here in Destiny's River and someday her heart would return there also."

"That's why you came here?"

"When Annie died, I was handed a letter from her via her attorney, Mr. Jacobs. She had never asked anything of me in all the years we lived together after she took me in off the streets. And when she died, she explained the missing parts of the story so I would understand what she was finally asking of me. She wanted to be brought back here. And she described the springs and that I would find a tree…a peach tree. And that is the spot she wanted her ashes spread. And then she would truly be at peace…at home."

"You brought her back here for that reason."

"This is the note that she left me. I think she says it better than I can."

Cade took the folded piece of paper from the envelope that had clearly been read and reread a few times. He surveyed its contents.

My darling little Ally girl,

If you are reading this, please do not cry. I know you will do so because you have a heart that is tender, and you are the one person I have shared my own memories and heart with these many years since I was blessed to have found you, and we became our own family. I ask one favor. Mr. Jacobs will explain how I have set forth the means of you taking on this request… Do not worry about the details. Although I know you will never change in that regard. But you and Teddy, who is now your family, will be okay. I leave knowing that in my heart.

My request is that you take me on a journey home. Take me back to where my heart was already buried years ago. There is a hill overlooking a valley… Wait until you see its beauty. And that is where the springs begin that flow downward through the valley to a beautiful river on which banks stand Destiny's River. I believe you will find it to be a place of beauty, good people, and peace. Peace is what I wish for you always. And to know a great love that will last a lifetime and beyond. Do not settle for less, my dear. And once you find your way to the spring, there is a tree, which I pray is still standing. If it is springtime, you will find it full of beautiful, fragrant blossoms. I do hope it still stands. And there, no ceremony, no fancy words…just love and peace and let the Texas breeze carry me over the place I never left in all my years. Then walk away and find your own grand adventure.

My heart will be with you always, and I am never far away.
Annie

Cade finished and slowly folded the letter and replaced it inside the envelope. He handed it back to Ally. "That explains so much. And I really don't know what to say. I wish things could have been different for them. But then so much would have been different for each of us."

"It was meant to be." Ally nodded. "Annie always said that. Everything happens for a reason, and we don't realize it at the time. But her and your grandfather's story has withstood time and now has come full circle."

"What had you planned? How were you going to do all this she asked?"

"I had no idea when I came. I knew there were springs. I was going to find a way to visit them—I know now they are open on certain days. And somehow, I would hope to find the tree and do what she wanted. But I hadn't planned the accident and all that has happened since that time. I was going to get my car running and be ready to leave and then I would do as she asked. Then that would free me to find that adventure she wished for me. I had to trust in her words."

"This area of the springs—this special area—is not open to the public. That is a deal that Tori and I made when she wanted to use the thermal springs for patients from the hospitals. The tree is here…not in bloom until spring…but let me show you where my grandfather told me he proposed."

They walked to the far side of the spring and a lone tree stood tall with many branches then bare due to the season. He walked to the side out of view and pointed upward. She joined him and then her breath caught in her throat. A heart had been carved just beneath the first branch. The initials inside it were: *J.C.L. loves A.D.P. 4 ever.*

"I wish she could have seen this herself," Ally said.

"I think she has." Cade nodded. "I think they both see it now…together." Silence surrounded them as the breeze blew over the hillside and down through the valley. *Peace.* There was peace.

Ally looked at Cade. He nodded. "You tell me when you want to do this, and I'll make it happen. I ask that you and whoever you need to be here attend along with Tori and my son. I think it would be fitting…that is if you would think Annie wouldn't mind that?"

Ally nodded. "I think she would agree. Love does prevail, and it does continue. She taught me that." She withdrew the necklace from around her neck. "There is one more thing. I think this belongs back with your family." She held out her palm and the ring lay in it. "It belongs to you and your future generations."

"No…it belongs right where it is," Cade said.

Ally lowered her hand. "Thank you. I'll keep it safe and then when I leave this world, it will come back to your children. Full circle."

Chapter Sixteen

"DID YOU HAVE fun? Weren't the horses amazing? I wish I could have gone with you." Ally was bombarded with Jillie's questions and comments about her day with the horses. But the truth wasn't to be shared. At least not yet. She and Cade agreed it would be told when Ally was ready for it and that would be when she was ready to leave.

"We need to concentrate on the festival. And if you don't hurry and get into costume, we'll be late," Ally reminded her, gathering up the bags of items she needed to take and then packing the cookies and pastries the class would sell. She wanted it all to go well as Tori was counting on her to do her job in her absence, and she wanted to make Jillie proud, as well as Matt and so many others. That was the time the phone had to ring. She answered it and her day just got worse. The music teacher had a stomach virus, and she needed someone to get the choir on stage and set and lead them. Ally had mentioned her experience with the church children's choir, and she could sing in tune. She had been to almost every rehearsal with Jillie…so the teacher begged her to do it. And the word no was something she needed to practice using more but it never was uttered. Now the clock was really ticking.

There was controlled chaos backstage when they arrived.

The choir had to be rounded up and nerves settled. Jillie had to get into costume. And the cookies needed to be delivered to the classroom. Matt sent a text that he was running late and was stuck at the office. Tori had yet to arrive with the baby and Ally knew that panic was not an option. She stepped in and began giving directions to those waiting for guidance. And the time struck the hour and the curtain was going up.

Ally had to hide her own nerves and pretend with a big smile. Somehow it worked. It all went by in a blur. The audience laughed during the parody of the first Thanksgiving dinner when they should, the songs went together and in tune, and the Fall Fest was kicked off in grand style. The applause was great. And when her name was called, she walked out from behind the curtain to be presented with a bouquet on behalf of the school along with two others and she was touched by their heartfelt thanks. And she caught sight of Tori giving her a thumbs-up in the audience and next to her was Cade smiling and clapping and then there was Matt. He was clapping harder than the rest and the smile he sent her was meant just for her. In that moment, she felt an incredible joy unlike anything she had known before. She belonged. What she felt she had lost in New York when Annie died, she had found in Destiny's River. How would she ever belong to any other place? But she kept the smile from fading as she walked offstage and then hugs came from the kids and a huge one from Jillie.

"You are the best ever, Miss Ally," the little girl said with a huge grin. "I was scared but I remembered what you said about the audience, and I just was able to do my part. I'm so glad you came here."

"That makes two of us." The voice belonged to a beaming Matt, and he joined them with some flowers for Jillie, and three roses for Ally to add to her bouquet-filled arms. "Congratulations! I hear word in the hall that they can't wait to see what you do next year."

Ally couldn't speak and luckily, she didn't have to do so. Tori came up and grabbed her into a hug. "I knew you could handle this. Way to go."

"Did you bring some of those pecan fudge things that I love?" Cade grinned and asked his most important question. Tori jabbed his arm.

"Go check out the classroom…and leave a big donation for all that you already ate while she made them," his wife reminded him.

"So, this is the amazing, talented, gifted, and beautiful Ally Jones," said a woman who stood with Tori. Ally had no idea who she was. Maybe someone who had come with Matt? She remembered seeing her standing next to him in the audience at the end.

The woman stuck out her hand and Ally automatically shook it. "I usually hug but since we haven't been introduced by any of these people standing here, I will shake hands. I'm the brilliant one of the family…Cassie Parker Connors. My husband and I just got back into town and he and my daughter, Emmie, are around here someplace. You'll meet them later."

"Did she say brilliant?" Matt leaned over and asked Tori, who looked as mystified as he did.

"She was out in that sun too long on the West Coast,"

Tori responded in kind. "Perhaps too much smog in the air, too."

"Don't pay attention to them," Cassie noted with an arched look in their direction. "They've always been jealous." She hooked her arm through Ally's, and she handed the flowers over to Matt. "Make yourself useful, little brother. Hold on to these. Ally and I are going to get acquainted while she takes me to where these amazing pastries are that I have heard so much about. Lead on, Ally."

☆

"AUNT CASSIE!" JILLIE left the table of cookies and launched herself into her aunt's arms. "I missed you! Where's Emmie?"

"I bet they're at the dunking booth trying to get the principal soaked, if I know them." Jillie gave her one more hug and left them in a whirl.

"So, what do you think of my brother and his little girl?" Cassie asked, her expression matching the sincerity of her question, while she bit into a sugar cookie decked out as a turkey with different-colored feathers. "Pretty cool, aren't they? And this cookie is amazing. So, what do you think of them?"

Ally could only stand in amazement at the rapid-fire way the woman's mind worked. She had heard that she was a special agent for law enforcement or some such, but she certainly had down the ability to interrogate and confuse.

"Cool, amazing, funny, adorable, and too generous."

"Which describes which of them?"

"You're a super sleuth, aren't you? You tell me." She bit

into her own cookie.

"I knew I liked you. The moment I saw that save where the turkey was losing his tail feather into the fan that cooled the choir and then it tipped toward the piano, but you grabbed the feathers and used that sneaky move with your foot to anchor the fan throughout that entire song. Great balance."

"Thank you, I think." Ally smiled. "You do see more than most."

"That's why I'm brilliant. But I let the others think they're special, too." They both shared a laugh and that's when she and Matt's other sister became friends.

"I like her," Cassie pronounced with a nod of her head in Ally's direction as the rest of the family gathered. "She can keep up with me. Unlike some in my own family."

"Jillie is with your bunch, and we need to get home to our son who is being watched over by Mrs. James and her husband. Joey was sleeping when it came time to dress, so we took advantage of the grandmother of ten who begged to watch him. But we miss him. Great going, Ally. Rest tomorrow and then we begin…rather *you* begin…to be roped into the Christmas Tree Celebration and all that entails… Good luck!" And she was gone before Ally could question her words.

"Funny how that works, isn't it? I felt that same shove in my backside when I moved back here and got married. I think a death certificate is the only way you get out of it. Or joining the army or some such. But we need to run too and unpack. I'll be seeing you soon!" She left after them.

"And that was the whirlwind of my family." Matt smiled

with a shake of his head. "Just imagine if my brother was in the mix, too. It can get crazy. But you fit right in."

"Are you saying I'm crazy in a backhanded sort of way?"

"Who me? Would I suggest that? I just mean you are a lady of many talents and the way you balanced that fan was incredible."

"No! You saw it, too? Did the whole audience see it?"

"Well, I know that the coach did, and he mentioned something about you coming over to the junior high and working your agility skills with his team."

Ally knew she was being had. "I suppose someone told you once that you have a sense of humor and are funny? I would ask for a second opinion if I were you." She smiled sweetly and began placing more cookies on the almost empty plates on the table.

Matt just shook his head and tried not to laugh. Somehow, she felt he might be planning some sort of retribution. He had that look about him. But he moved off to try the roulette wheel in the fifth-grade classroom.

The Fall Fest had been a success by all accounts. Ally had received so many kind comments that had her smiling all evening. She had helped this community in some small way and that made her feel connected to them. She was packing up when a text came across her phone. It was from Matt. He had been called out into the country on an emergency with his deputy. He hated to not be there to help close up. But he would make it up to her. And left it at that.

It would have been nice to finish up and have someone besides Teddy to listen to her account of the evening. Someone to share the feeling of success with. Instead, she cleaned up the kitchen where she had rushed earlier to bake the last of the cookies and left things out of place. Then she put on her nightgown and robe and settled into the comfy chair next to the fireplace. Maybe tomorrow she would figure out how to set a fire in the fireplace. That would be nice on the fall evenings that were becoming chillier.

So much had happened in such a short amount of time. Ally thought back over it all. She was amazed at how much she had gone from stranger to being praised for helping the community's school and making friends like Tillie at the café. Helping the choir teacher and Jillie's homeroom teacher with their classes and funding for school supplies thanks to a successful festival. She enjoyed every moment. Teddy was able to receive great vet care and was walking better already. Her car would be repaired soon, and she had found a way to have two jobs and save so much more money. Mr. Jacobs had sent her an email that morning to tell her that the papers would be ready to close on the apartment within two weeks. She would be able to pay all her other bills, including medical. And have the nest egg left that Annie had insured for her.

The only thing left would be to pay the debt Matt had shouldered for her. Even though he did not want repayment, she knew she had to make it right with herself. She had put it off because of the debt and because of the need to figure out how and when to put Annie to rest. Cade had stepped up and that detail would be handled. So all that was really left was how to say goodbye. It wouldn't be so hard a task to even think about if she hadn't allowed herself to get involved in the life of the small town, to like the people, and to even feel more than she should about Jillie and her dad—Matt. That was a subject she had danced around for a while. She had no problem being a buffer between him and the women in the town…get them to back off a while. But she would leave and then he would have the problem return. Unless someone else stepped into her shoes—and there were those like Frannie who would be happy to see her go.

She had allowed herself to get caught up in the dream…and ignored the reality. Primrose Inn had become the home she had never had but had been a dream. Tori had spread magic in the place she had found to make a home for herself and her siblings. And it had sprinkled some into her world, too. The people in town had become her friends. They had let her carve out a spot for herself and they welcomed her without question. How would she and Teddy find such a place when they leave? What if they stayed? Nothing would change, or would it? She could find a small apartment. They couldn't stay in Primrose Inn. That belonged to Tori and her family. She could continue with the pastries and pies and such for the café and maybe expand to other places in the area with a commercial license. She'd have to find a second job because Tori would be back to picking up Jillie after school. Even if she didn't, Ally needed to distance herself. Matt wouldn't always be ignoring the women in town trying to catch his eye. One day, one would come along, and she knew she didn't want to be watching from the outside. Because she had grown too close to Matt.

He was a good man and a great dad, and he cared about so many in his town. He was a large part of its very fabric. He deserved someone special. Someone that was not her. It would be someone who had a normal childhood, not the streets of New York. A person who fit into a big family and has ties and a history here. That is who he deserved.

She would do her best to decide how to make the transition in the coming days and be ready to move to another town hopefully by Christmas. She didn't want to go through the holidays, still unsure of her future or her place in it. But first she would need to put Annie where she wanted to be. And she felt blessed to be part of a great love story, even if it wasn't hers.

Chapter Seventeen

"GIVE. WHAT'S THE story?"

Matt looked up from his plate of food and tried to guess what Cassie was talking about. "Story as in…?"

"The one where you are using a beautiful, sweet girl as a shield to hide behind from all the single women who want to apply for the job of being Mrs. Parker. Is that plain enough?"

"You should ask Tori. It was one of her ideas that just took on a life of its own. And Ally wants to pay me back for helping get her car fixed. It was our fault the accident happened at all… And she wants to pay for her dog's leg surgery…again part of the accident. She insists on repaying me. Once that's done, then she leaves."

"And I hear that she found a second job because she's also one heck of a great baker, and she's helping out with Jillie while Tori is out of commission. She has a strong work ethic. Jillie clearly adores her. She fits right into this town with that festival as an example. So, what is stopping you?"

"Stopping me?"

"Have you always been so obtuse? How do you solve the crimes around here? I know you are a lot smarter than this. Or is it just because it involves someone who has finally broken through that heart of yours and made you wake up? And being a typical man, it has you running scared."

"I'm not running scared from anything."

"Ally Jones. Do you like her or not?"

"Why don't we change the subject?"

"See? You're running and that proves my point."

"What are you trying to prove?"

"She plans to leave when her debt is paid…yes or no?"

"Yes."

"Does she have a plan as to where she's moving on to?"

"Not that I've heard."

"Why does she need to leave a place where it's so easy for her to put down roots?"

"Maybe she wants to see something different. I don't know, ask her."

"If you don't, I will."

"Stay out of it, Cassie."

"Now you know better than to tell me that. And one last question…do you want her to stay—yes or no?"

Matt didn't respond as quickly as he had to the other questions. He met his sister's gaze with his steady one. Then he spoke. "Yes."

Cassie smiled. And she nodded. "That's really the only answer that matters then, isn't it? And I think you need to figure out the why of it. Why should she want to stay? Seems like you need to step out from hiding behind her and make your intention known to this town but also to her. You want her to stay, then give her the reason to do so. And if you can't do that now, then let her go." She stood from the table. "Good luck, little brother. I'll put this counseling session on your bill."

Matt shook his head as he watched her leave. It had always been Cassie to stir the pot and put things in perspective. She could be maddening at times, but then she was also right…most of the time. He knew that the clock was ticking on Ally's leaving. He'd tried to ignore it. But it was coming. Jillie had also sensed it. She had asked him why Ally had to leave at all. Did she not like it in Destiny's River? Maybe she was regretting leaving the big city? Destiny's River was a great place to live but not everyone could leave a large city and take the change of pace. But Ally had never struck him as that type. She had come in and from the beginning fit into the town…into their lives. She had the heart for Destiny's River. The question was, could she have the heart to want to stay? Heart to want to take on him and his daughter and their lives? He was a small-town sheriff. He chose this life and not too many women would want to make such a decision. A decision that affected three people. He wanted nothing less than a lifetime commitment. Not too many women thought that far, or so it seemed from his experience.

Ally had pitched in above and beyond. She knew the meaning of commitment and teamwork. It had been tough to convince Jillie of the sincerity of the few dates he had gone through in the past. And none had made it very far in her eyes or in his estimation. Until Ally Jones literally crashed into their lives. Nothing had been the same since. And it was time he focused on what might change her mind and get her to consider staying. Because he wanted her to do just that. It might take some work, but he would give it his best shot. She needed to know that she was wanted. That she had become part of their lives, and she would be missed if she left. And he didn't want that to happen.

He had his work cut out for him. The lady in question was about to know what happened when a Parker put their mind to something.

Ally pulled into the driveway and parked. She had delivered the café's order and then drove around a bit, meeting the other business owners and spreading the word that she was available. The wedding shop was very interested in seeing what baking she could do for weddings. And that would be an area she would focus on honing her talents to include that avenue. She had also visited the garage and saw the work was moving along on her car. It would get a paint job in the coming week and that was exciting.

She gathered her purse and a small bag of fruit she had picked up at the farmer's market and headed up the steps to the porch. She stopped and wasn't sure she was in the right place for a moment. On the doormat sat a huge bouquet of gold mums, yellow glads, tiny orange buttons, greenery and deep maroon gerberas. They were beautiful fall colors, and it had to be a mistake. The delivery person needed to be called. She saw a small envelope and retrieved it to get the name of the florist to call. But she stopped when she saw that it was her name printed on the envelope. It wasn't a mistake after all. She drew out the card from inside. And her breath caught in her throat for a moment.

Good morning, beautiful lady. Hope these flowers bring a smile. Would you do Jillie and me the honor of joining us for Thanksgiving dinner at the Lockwood Ranch? Everyone would love to have you with us. Pick you up at eleven. Matt

Ally felt a rush of excitement. No one had ever sent her flowers. And such gorgeous ones! And she was invited for a family Thanksgiving. It felt special. And Matt had invited her. She needed to respond. Once she had opened the door and set the bouquet on the low table in the center of the living room and dropped the rest of her things in the kitchen she dialed Matt, wondering at the butterflies in her stomach. She talked to the man daily, but he had never sent her flowers or called her beautiful. Something had changed.

He answered on the third ring. "Good morning. How are you today?"

"Very surprised. And yes, I am smiling…quite a lot. The flowers are incredible. Thank you for them."

"I'm glad they brought smiles, and that you like them. You deserve them."

"I called to thank you but also to accept your kind invitation for lunch."

"I'm glad. I'll pick you up at eleven."

"What can I bring? I want to do something."

"Well, since you offered." He laughed. "I do have a request from my brother-in-law."

She couldn't help smiling. "Let me guess…pecan fudge brownies. Surely, I can bring something else, too?"

"Coconut cream pie might be a hit. Of course, you could just surprise us. Because anything you bake is amazing."

It made her heart feel good to hear his words. "Then I will surprise everyone. And I'll be ready at eleven."

"Can't wait. Enjoy the day off today and we'll see you Thursday. Bye, Ally."

She managed to get out a bye in return and hung up. She

was smiling so much that her jaws hurt. It was flowers and a dinner invitation, but it meant so much more to her. And he had to know it would. He was a man who had a lot of empathy and caring for people. And he knew she would be alone. He and his family were making sure that did not happen. But he had also called her beautiful. And for the first time, she felt it. Maybe this bit of a dream would become a possible reality. At least for one day, she would allow herself to entertain that dream.

☆

"TEDDY, IT'S THANKSGIVING! And you get extra treats today after you finish your breakfast. I'm going out but there will be another treat when I get home."

Ally felt the butterflies again. And she caught herself humming. When had she ever done that? She searched her closet and changed three times. She finally settled on burgundy slacks with a lighter burgundy sweater shot through with thin silver threads. Would it be too dressy or not dressy enough? She had to hope for the best. She took extra time with her makeup and her curls were their usual bouncy selves. She longed for straight hair like other girls, but it was not going to happen. Pale pink lip gloss went on just as the doorbell sounded. The butterflies really took flight.

Matt stood on the doorstep. He was dressed in pressed brown slacks, with a crisp beige linen shirt under a brown corduroy jacket. Polished boots shone on his feet and his hat was in his hand. It was what was in his other hand that caught her attention. A large bone wrapped in cellophane with a red bow on top. His grin held a bit of mischief.

"I thought since you had flowers already that Teddy might be feeling left out. So, this might entertain him for a while." He handed her the bone as she stepped back to let him come inside.

"It is certainly a first, but it is perfect. Teddy will love it. Thank you. And I have the boxes of desserts in the kitchen if you want to move them to your truck. I'll get my jacket."

They were soon on the road. The sun was shining, and the sky was a vivid blue. The temperature was in the lower sixties with a breeze. It was a perfect day. Ally had a feeling it also had a lot to do with the man beside her. She decided it was a dream kind of day and she settled back into the leather seat and found the smiles just kept coming.

"Jillie's at Cassie's house. They should be over for lunch by noon. We have a lot to be thankful for this year."

"Yes, it's been quite a year," she agreed. "So many changes. But most for the good."

"I know you lost someone you loved. And you had to leave a comfort zone that you knew to come all the way out here. I have to be selfish and say that despite all of that, I'm glad you did come to Destiny."

"In spite of everything, I have to admit that it was still a year with things to be thankful for. And coming here and meeting your family and Jillie…and you, made it possible to manage it."

"I'm glad I was included in that list." He smiled and she returned it. They turned in the entrance and soon were being greeted by Cade who came out to help them carry the desserts.

"I can't wait until the end of the meal." He smiled, noting the box labeled with his favorites inside. "Perhaps we should do a taste test beforehand."

"Don't you dare touch those desserts," came a warning voice from the kitchen, which he led them into. Tori was standing keeping an eye on her husband. He sat the boxes down and then nodded to Matt. "We better leave now while we can. When your sister gets that look…"

"I am well acquainted with it, so let's go," Matt agreed, and they left the kitchen.

"I'm so glad you could come," Tori said, giving her a quick hug. "Matt and Jillie were happy when you said you would."

"I'm grateful to be included."

"I smell something wonderful," came the voice approaching down the hall, and then Cassie appeared with a casserole in hand. "The gang has arrived. Let the party begin."

And it did. Ally couldn't remember laughing so much in a long time. The food was amazing. And she met Cassie's husband, Cole, and her stepdaughter, Emmie, who was about the same age as Jillie.

"I wish Rance could have joined us," Tori said, a wistful smile on her face. "But he's on some assignment far from here. He called earlier to wish all a happy Thanksgiving."

"The table is growing and that's a great sign," Cassie said looking around at everyone. "I think we should give thanks, each of us, for something."

"I like that," Tori said. "I'll start. I am most thankful for an amazing husband who puts up with me—" a great laugh followed on that note "—and for the gift of a beautiful, healthy son. What more could a person want?"

"I echo on my wife's thanks for our son and for her gracing my life." And the smile he sent her way made Ally melt. "But I am also thankful for a special visitor who came along and brought an unexpected piece of a missing puzzle in my family. I asked for permission earlier to share this story with you. It is a love story...the kind we all seek. It is happy and it is sad, but it has now come full circle."

He unfolded the piece of note paper and cleared his throat and began. "Once upon a time, a young boy and young girl fell in love beneath the peach tree at the springs here on this ranch. But their love could never be. So, the young girl left behind the ring he had given to her and went far away. He searched for her but only to return the thing that would always be hers. With his heart. He married another woman who added riches to this land we stand on today. But his heart was far away in a big city. The years passed. He died. Then the day came when she died also. But she had asked a very special woman to bring her ashes back to the place she left her heart. And this young lady did just that. I realized this story when I saw the ring that my grandfather had given to his one and only love all those years before around the neck of Ally Jones." All gazes fell on her.

"Ally and I went to the springs, and we have decided that it is fitting to honor those wishes and bring the two hearts together again." There was silence around the table as people digested the unexpected news. And looks cast Ally's way once again. But they were kind looks and huge smiles.

"To that end, Ally and I are planning a special moment where that wonderful woman who held my grandfather's heart so long can be put to rest on their hill. It will be simple per her request and just the people around this table are invited to join, if you wish. Thank you, Ally, from the bottom of my heart—and my grandfather's, I am certain."

"Ally, you're next," Jillie said. "What are you grateful for?"

"I'm not one to do a lot of speaking, but from my heart, I am thankful for each and every person who opened their arms and hearts and welcomed me into the beauty of Destiny's River and the warmth and spirit of those who live here. I am forever grateful to Annie for asking me to come here. I think she was still guiding me by doing that. She wanted me to come here and see what she always knew. And to each of you, my thanks don't seem enough, but they are heartfelt."

"I'm thankful for my dad and all he does for me and others," Jillie began. "And thankful that Ally and Teddy came to Destiny. I'd be grateful if they would stay forever."

There were smiles and interesting looks being sent toward Matt. He was up to the task. "I'm grateful for my daughter, my family, my health, and my community. And I will echo my daughter in thanking Ally for coming here. For taking care of Jillie and working to make the school's festival successful for all the children who go there. And I hope that this time next year we're all here around this table and grateful that Ally is still with us."

Cassie coughed and took a sip of her tea. Tori winked at him. Cade nodded. Ally seemed locked on a design on the tablecloth. She had to process. And she had to act normally. Whatever that was.

She was truly grateful when Cassie went next, and the

rest followed. The atmosphere picked up again with laughter when the desserts were served. Everyone found at least one dessert that was a favorite. Jillie had her favorite pumpkin pie, and she hugged Ally's neck for remembering.

Ally had the pleasure of sitting in a rocking chair later and getting acquainted with the newest member of the clan. She only had experience with babies on Sundays at the church in New York where she would help with the infants. That was the extent of it. But she found Joey was a calm baby and he seemed to have some interest in watching her watching him.

"You are a natural," Tori said, smiling as she sat nearby.

"He makes me look good," Ally responded.

"Well, it's time he gets his dinner and then his nap, or he won't look good at all." Tori took him in her arms, and they bid all goodbyes. It was time to head home. Matt was covering the evening so his deputies could be with their families. Jillie was going home with her cousin to Cassie's again.

Ally gave a final wave to her hosts as she and Matt drove away. It was mostly a silent drive back into town. Matt had put on some music and Ally was okay with that. She had a lot to think about.

Matt walked with her to her front door. She wasn't sure how that part of the day was going to go. So, she was about to thank him again when he spoke first.

"I hope you didn't feel that you were put on the spot at dinner. I'm glad though that Cade explained what was going on with his grandfather and Annie. It was indeed a miracle that brought you here the more I think about it. I would like to be there at the ceremony."

"I'm glad. It would be nice to have you there. And I didn't feel put on the spot. It was a bit of a surprise maybe, but not in a bad way."

"Good," he said, and his hand found hers and she felt such warmth and peace in having hers in his.

"This is uncharted territory for me," he began. "I've gone on dates before. But nothing of any importance came from them. I guess I gave up and was irritated by unwanted attention. Jillie and I got through the years since she lost her mother. I was afraid of making the wrong choice where she was concerned. So, I did nothing. And then you crashed into our lives." He grinned at his own words. "Quite literally. And it seemed natural…like you fit in without any warning. I still tried to hold that wall in place that had gone up along the way over time. But you just 'fit'…in so many ways. I guess I'm not very good at saying this but to put it simply I want to date you. I want to have more time to figure out what you want and if you would even be interested in staying in a small town. I'm not good at saying what I want to say and you…"

Ally did what she wanted for the first time in her life totally on impulse. She went up on tiptoe and silenced his fumbling words with her lips. And to her surprise and pleasure, Matt took it from there, folding his arms around her and holding her close while his lips took the lead. And in that moment, there was no solid ground beneath her, her eyes closed and the porch was floating around her—or was she floating around the porch? The sensation was incredible. And for once she hoped the dream had become an absolute reality.

Matt drew back a little and he had a dazed look about him, but then a slow smile appeared, and his gaze was filled with an incredible light. "I do like how you cut to the bottom line and get to the heart of the matter."

"I never have done anything like that in my life."

"I think you should feel free to do it more often…on one condition."

"One condition?"

"That I get to do the same thing…to move the conversation along when needed."

"I think that's only fair."

His grin was wide and beautiful. "I think I'd better say good night as duty does call. And for once, I would gladly skip it."

"No, you won't. That's not the Matt Parker I know. But you can pick up that conversation at a later date."

"I like your thinking." The next kiss was even better than the first. "Good night and sweet dreams."

He waited until she shut the door behind her, and it locked. She didn't remember walking up the stairs or anything much after that. But she did dream…and it was the best dream ever.

Chapter Eighteen

THREE WEEKS HAD passed. And Matt had taken dating to a new level. They went to restaurants, a couple of dances; she helped him with the planning of the tree-lighting ceremony on the square. They watched movies with popcorn on the couch along with Jillie...and sometimes without her. She helped shop for gifts for his family and for Jillie. And then as she watched the tall tree lit with its hundreds of lights, returned greetings with so many more people she had met in Destiny, and found the many places Matt had found to place mistletoe, that a thought hit her.

I love Christmas!

How much difference a year had made in her feelings about the holidays. And it had come because Annie had told her stories of a place called Destiny's River. And she had sent her on her last request to come back to that town. The day had come.

The small group gathered on top of the hill on the Lockwood Ranch. The day was cold, but the sun shone. They had decided on the hour before sunset because that was Annie's favorite part of the day. She had said that was when Joseph had proposed. There was a prayer by the Parkers' pastor. 'Amazing Grace'—her favorite hymn—was sung. And Cade reiterated the love story between his grandfather and the love of his life. That was when the small box was opened, and the breeze seemed to cooperate. Annie's ashes floated free over the side of the hill and then higher across the valley toward the setting sun. Cade had shared with her earlier that his grandfather had a headstone in the family cemetery, but his ashes had been set free right before sunset in the same spot years before. Ally liked to think he was there waiting to soar with his love at last. Her tears were joyful at that moment. She had grieved tears of sadness when Annie left her. Now, all she could feel was grateful and happy for the woman who gave her the map to find her own true love. The others moved back down the hill to meet at the house. But she and Matt remained.

He had her hand safe and warm in his. His strength had been beside her the whole time.

She watched the sun blazing just above the horizon. Then Matt moved to capture her other hand and bring her gaze to his.

"I've tried to think of what the perfect moment would be to say this to you. And I couldn't seem to find the perfect way. Until now. I believe that things are set in motion long before they happen. I think Annie sending you here was an example of that. Because of her great love, she sent you here to be mine. I love you, Ally Jones. From the first moment I laid eyes on you in the hospital. I can't explain it. It was like I had been waiting. And you finally came. Being a man, it took me a little while to understand that fact. But when I did, I knew I would move heaven and earth to keep you in Destiny's River. It was destiny that brought you here to a town of the same name. I'm hoping you'll understand why this is the perfect time and place."

And still holding her hands, he sank to one knee. Ally was frozen in total surprise. "Ally Jones, please stay with me in Destiny's River for the rest of our lives and write our own great love story each and every day we have together. Will you marry me?"

Ally felt incredible peace fill her and circle them both. It was as light as a gentle hug, but she knew from where it came. She looked into the eyes of her one and only love and knew destiny had indeed brought her home.

The End

If you enjoyed *The Sheriff's Mistletoe Bride*,
you'll love the other books in…

Destiny's River Series

Book 1: *Home to the Cowboy's Arms*

Book 2: *The Rancher's Fake Fiancée*

Book 3: *The Sheriff's Mistletoe Bride*

Available now at your favorite online retailer!

More Books by Debra Holt

Texas Heritage series

Book 1: *The Texas Cowboy's Proposal*
Book 2: *The Texas Cowboy's Lady*
Book 3: *The Texas Cowboy's Rescue*
Book 4: *The Texas Cowboy's Christmas Miracle*

The Tremaynes of Texas series

Book 1: *Capturing the Texas Rancher's Heart*
Book 2: *The Rancher Risks It All*
Book 3: *The Bronc Rider Takes a Fall*
Book 4: *The Sheriff and the Cowgirl*

The Blood Brothers series

Book 1: *True Blue Cowboy*
Book 2: *Homeward Bound, Cowboy*
Book 3: *Her Secret Cowboy*

The Texas Lawmen series

Book 1: *Beware the Ranger*
Book 2: *The Lawman's Apache Moon*
Book 3: *Along Came a Ranger*
Book 4: *The Sheriff's Christmas Angels*

Available now at your favorite online retailer!

About the Author

Born and raised in the Lone Star state of Texas, Debra grew up among horses, cowboys, wide open spaces, and real Texas Rangers. Pride in her state and ancestry knows no bounds and it is these heroes and heroines she loves to write about the most. She also draws upon a variety of life experiences including working with abused children, caring for baby animals at a major zoo, and planning high-end weddings (ah, romance!).

Debra's real pride and joys, however, are her son, an aspiring film actor, and a daughter with aspirations to join the Federal Bureau of Investigation. (more story ideas!) When she isn't busy writing about tall Texans and feisty heroines, she can be found cheering on her Texas Tech Red Raiders, or heading off on another cruise adventure. She read her first romance…Janet Dailey's Fiesta San Antonio, over thirty years ago and became hooked on the genre. Writing contemporary western romances, is both her passion and dream come true, and she hopes her books will bring smiles…and sighs…to all who believe in happily-ever-after's.

Thank you for reading

The Sheriff's Mistletoe Bride

If you enjoyed this book, you can find more from all our great authors at TulePublishing.com, or from your favorite online retailer.

TULE
PUBLISHING

Printed in Dunstable, United Kingdom

69103222R00122